"We can't go on like this...."

"Hush, sweetheart." Seth placed one loving finger against Margo's mouth. "I planned to save this, but I've never been more sure of anything. I want to marry you, Margo."

Margo wasn't sure if it was the biting salt spray making her eyes water so, or tears of mingled happiness and regret. "Oh, Seth," she moaned. "You know it would never work. Your daughter..."

"Hasn't been this happy since I got divorced. Our getting together will be the best thing that's ever happened to her."

Unbidden, the idea that she could have both Seth *and* the daughter she'd lost at birth took root in Margo's heart. The only price she'd have to pay was silence. And the loss of her self-respect. For she would be building their marriage on a lie.

Dear Reader,

August is vacation month, and no matter where you're planning to go, don't forget to take along this month's Silhouette Romance novels. They're the perfect summertime read! And even if you can't get away, you can still escape from it all for a few hours of love and adventure with Silhouette Romance books.

August continues our WRITTEN IN THE STARS series. Each month in 1992 we're proud to present a book that focuses on the hero and his astrological sign. This month we're featuring the proud, passionate Leo man in Suzanne Carey's intensely emotional *Baby Swap*.

You won't want to miss the rest of our fabulous August lineup. We have love stories by Elizabeth August, Brittany Young, Carol Grace and Carla Cassidy. As a special treat, we're introducing a talented newcomer, Sandra Paul. And in months to come, watch for Silhouette Romance novels by many more of your favorite authors, including Diana Palmer, Annette Broadrick and Marie Ferrarella.

The Silhouette Romance authors and editors love to hear from readers and we'd love to hear from *you*.

Happy reading from all of us at Silhouette!

Valerie Susan Hayward
Senior Editor

SUZANNE CAREY

Baby Swap

Published by Silhouette Books New York

America's Publisher of Contemporary Romance

With love and thanks to my good friend Phyllis O'Bryan
of PMD Counseling in Largo, Florida, whose skills as an
astrologer and psychic were a tremendous help to me in
fleshing out the characters for this book.

SILHOUETTE BOOKS
300 E. 42nd St., New York, N.Y. 10017

BABY SWAP

ISBN: 0-373-08880-9

First Silhouette Books printing August 1992

SUZANNE CAREY

I used to read my horoscope only when I was depressed or worried. Then my good friend Phyllis O'Bryan, a top psychic and astrologer of the Tampa Bay area, changed all that. I met Phyllis while doing a feature on Halley's Comet.

I went to Phyllis when I began writing this book. I gave her a Leo man, the characters' ages and the story I had in mind. Selecting Gemini for the heroine's sign because of the strong attraction between Leo and Gemini, she did natal charts for the hero, heroine and both daughters.

Phyllis says she found the process fascinating. I'm grateful for her generous, enthusiastic and knowledgeable support.

One postscript: as a Libra, I was surprised at how closely the Leo-Gemini interaction fit my relationship with my Leo husband. Just for fun, Phyllis did my chart. Both my rising and moon signs turned out to be Gemini!

LEO

Fifth sign of the Zodiac
July 23 to August 22
Symbol: Lion
Planet: Sun
Element: Fire
Stone: Ruby
Color: Yellow, Orange
Metal: Gold
Flower: Gladiolus
Lucky Day: Sunday
Countries: France, Italy, Czechoslovakia
Cities: Chicago, Rome, Miami

Famous Leos

Alfred Hitchcock
Napoleon Bonaparte
Peter Jennings
Patrick Swayze

Jacqueline Kennedy Onassis
Madonna
Whitney Houston
Amelia Earhart

Prologue

The tall, redheaded man with blond eyebrows was back. He stood looking through the double-glass pane like an overgrown boy peering through a toy store window, his gaze fastened hungrily on one small, downy head. His child was Baby Girl Danner, according to the pink-and-white card attached to her crib. She'd been in the nursery at Bayless Memorial since the first time Margo had put on her flowery quilted robe and walked down the hall to check on Beth Ann.

Funny, she thought. He's got a new baby and he obviously cares a great deal about her. Yet he looks as unhappy as I feel. Seconds later she conceded he was probably as ecstatic as a lark. He just hid it well. She was projecting her heavy load of conflicting emotions onto him.

Happy. Sad. Frightened. Loving. When it came to her inner woman, God knew, all those feelings and more

were churning perilously near the surface. Too fre-
quently these days, they spilled over in the form of tears.

At the moment, happiness was uppermost. Pressing
her face against the glass, Margo focused with a rush of
maternal affection on the tiny, perfect fingers of Baby
Girl Rourke as they fluttered like butterflies' wings at a
sudden sound.

"Beth Ann Rourke," she whispered. "You'll never
know how much you are wanted."

It was one of life's miracles that, though he'd already
been fighting a rare form of cancer at the time of Beth's
conception, Jim had given Margo a baby. Now Margo
had reciprocated, returning to him one of life's most
precious gifts.

Before it was too late.

Jim's cancer was getting worse. Though the doctors
tried to hold out hope, Margo could tell they were somewhat discouraged. Little Beth Ann, so pretty and delicate looking now that the deep rosy flush of birth had
faded, would be his immortality. His contribution to the
next generation. And the one after that.

Unfortunately, he hadn't seen his daughter yet. He'd
had to report for chemotherapy at Swedish Hospital's
Fred Hutchinson Cancer Research Center the day before
Margo's labor pains had started. A public relations
staffer at Bayless before going on maternity leave, she'd
gone there for the birth because of a sizable employee
discount. As a result, they were stuck in separate hospi-
tals a few blocks apart on Seattle's First Hill, sometimes
called "Pill Hill" because of its heavy concentration of
medical facilities.

Nell Hafner, who was one of Jim's regular nurses at
Fred Hutchinson and a neighbor of theirs in the city's

Ravenna district, was waiting for Margo when she returned to her room.

"How's my hubby?" Margo asked, anxiety regaining the upper hand. "I phoned him around lunchtime, and he wasn't feeling too well then."

"By the time I went off duty, a little better, I think. He's really anxious to see you and the baby."

Parking her purse on the floor, Nell sank into the squeaky brown leatherette visitor's chair. She'd brought a pen, a clipboard with some sheets of paper attached to it and a couple of paperbound books. The one on top was labeled *Ephimeris*. Both had faded blue covers.

Margo kicked off her slippers and got back into bed. She and Nell had become fast friends during the long months of Jim's treatment and she felt comfortable in her presence. Arranging her unruly dark curls so they wouldn't be crushed flat by leaning against the pillow, she smiled at the older woman. Life went on. You couldn't panic from moment to moment.

"What's that stuff for?" she asked.

"We were going to do your chart, remember?"

"Oh. Right."

A skilled nurse in her professional life, Nell had an elderly aunt who'd been an astrologer. The aunt had passed on her craft as someone might bequeath a treasure. As a result, for quite a few of her forty-three years, Nell had dabbled in the science of the stars.

It definitely wasn't a game to her. Whereas Margo tended to thumb through astrology magazines at her supermarket newsstand whenever she was depressed and then laugh at their predictions, Nell took the pull of the stars on human lives quite seriously.

Margo shrugged inwardly as the nurse brought out a blank, photocopied chart that resembled a wheel with spokes. Letting her do my chart can't hurt, she thought. If nothing else, it will prove distracting. She didn't want to admit she was just the tiniest bit afraid of what she might be about to hear.

"So," Nell said, her gray eyes as intent as they always were when she immersed herself in her favorite topic, "you were born on June 4, 1961, right? At 5:23 p.m.?"

Margo nodded. "Right so far."

"That means you're a Gemini, which you already know. It's the sign of duality, twinship and many changes. With your Uranus in Leo, they could be unexpected . . . literally 'out of the blue.'"

Margo was skeptical. "It's certainly true about the changes," she admitted. "There've been plenty of those. But the twinship part is way off the mark. I'm an only child. My parents died when I was quite young. I never had a sibling, let alone an alter ego."

Her friendly nurse-astrologer was not to be deterred. "Perhaps the twinship factor has to do with your personality," she speculated. "Or some situation in your life that hasn't manifested itself yet.

"At the time of your birth, your sun was in the eighth house. That particular house is ruled by Scorpio. Hence, you're concerned with transition and union, life, death, regeneration."

Though she winced at the word death, Margo decided to go with the flow. Nell had already told her that, in a chart, death didn't have to be taken literally. Like its counterpart in the Tarot deck, it might refer to separation followed by reunion, a new beginning. She relaxed a little more and allowed her mind to run in unaccustomed channels as Nell continued.

"Scorpio rising tends to counteract what could otherwise have been a somewhat flighty nature. You're intense, persistent, even dogged, the type to dig for facts and investigate behind-the-scene events. If you're frustrated, you keep on digging, until you find what you're looking for.

"Both your moon and Jupiter are in Aquarius, making you creative and outgoing, thus balancing your somewhat introverted side. With your Mars in Leo, you have a healthy self-esteem...."

As she listened, Margo took Nell's comments with a grain of salt. They seemed to apply. But then again, the descriptions might have fit anyone. She hesitated when Nell offered to take a stab at her daily horoscope.

"Happiness over Beth Ann. Worries about Jim," she said. "That's all it's going to show."

"On the contrary." Nell appeared to check her facts and concluded that she'd interpreted them correctly. "From the positions of the stars today vis-à-vis your natal chart," she revealed, "I'd have to say a rather significant event has happened, or will happen today. You've met...or will meet...someone who will change your life. Leo might be involved."

Margo laughed. It felt good to let some of the worry and tension drain out of her body. "You're off by a day!" she teased, her dark eyes flashing with humor as she caught Nell in what had to be one of several obvious errors. "The someone you're talking about is Beth. And she's a Sagittarius."

Chapter One

Margo was tense, her nerves at the breaking point as she waited for private detective Harry Spence to give her the results of his investigation. She'd lost a lot over the past eight years—her husband, Jim in 1984 and, more recently, in 1991, her seven-year-old daughter in a school bus accident. But maybe, if the genetic study she'd allowed Beth Ann to participate in a few weeks before her death was valid, Margo hadn't lost everything. Maybe she still *had* a daughter.

The nationwide study, which would track its subjects for years, sought to determine whether there was an inherited predisposition to the rare form of cancer Jim had. With the slides of Jim's tissue long since frozen for their research, scientists had requested an infinitesimally small sample—a few cells, really—from one of Beth Ann's fingertips. It hadn't seemed much to ask. There'd been a quick prick, followed by smiles and a lollipop for Beth.

Incredibly, though, the small act of cooperation had up-ended Margo's world.

As far from the movie stereotype of a gumshoe as it was humanly possible for anyone to be, Harry Spence shuffled some papers. "No guarantees, Mrs. Rourke," he said in his dry, sandpapery voice. "But I may have found what you're looking for. At the time of Beth Ann's birth, there was only one other baby girl of Caucasian ancestry in the Bayless Memorial nursery. She and Beth Ann were born on the same day, six hours and twenty-three minutes apart."

Margo stared. She hadn't expected the facts to be so cut and dried, so easily sorted. If there'd been several possible candidates...

"Her name is Susan Lynn Danner. Her parents were divorced a year and a half ago. She still lives here in Seattle—the Magnolia section, to be precise—with her father, Seth Danner. He's a custom yacht builder, in partnership with his brother."

"And her mother?"

"Remarried and living in Hawaii. According to the court records, she didn't seek custody."

Margo digested the information. Her skin was prickling with little shivers that had nothing to do with the temperature. "What else can you tell me about the child?" she asked. "Is she happy? Well?"

Sympathy flickered in Harry Spence's colorless eyes. "As for 'happy,' Mrs. Rourke, I couldn't say. From what I could tell, she seems healthy enough. However, there *is* something else that might interest you..."

A thousand thoughts competed in Margo's head as the detective explained that Seth Danner had placed an ad for a housekeeper. It had run in the previous Sunday's paper.

"He's looking for somebody to live-in a minimum of five days a week," he said. "Cook, clean, watch over the girl when she comes home from school. I had my secretary phone and pass herself off as a potential applicant. It seems they've had a parade of people in that post since Danner's divorce...most of them unsatisfactory. Currently, an elderly baby-sitter is holding down the fort in the afternoons. Danner's interviewing at his boat yard office. If you went, it's not likely you'd get a look at the child unless he was serious about hiring you."

He passed a photograph across the desk. Obviously enlarged, it had the grainy texture characteristic of shots taken with high-speed film and a telephoto lens. The face that looked back at Margo from what appeared to be a school playground might have been her own when she was eight or nine years old.

But Beth favored me, she thought, still unwilling to accept the unexpected turn of events. *Not as much as this girl does,* her truthful inner self replied.

Shortly after Beth Ann's accident, the researchers had approached Margo again. To their surprise, the girl's tissue hadn't matched Jim's. As testing was 99.999995 percent accurate, they'd murmured, it wasn't very likely that she was his child. Had paternity ever been in question?

It most definitely had *not,* Margo had assured them. Still, mystified after she'd cooled down, she'd submitted a tissue sample of her own. And the result had been the same. The proteins in Beth's cell coatings hadn't matched hers, either. In their cool, detached way, the researchers had informed her that Beth couldn't possibly have been *her* biological daughter.

The researchers' findings had been quite a shock. If the unthinkable *had* happened and the child she'd borne Jim

Rourke had inadvertently been switched for that of another woman, Margo wasn't sure she would be able to make herself believe it. To do so would mean Beth Ann hadn't really been theirs. It would be like losing her all over again.

Yet, what if the baby she'd carried beneath her heart for nine long months was living just a few miles away, growing up and celebrating birthday after birthday without her? What would she do? How could she find out if the girl Harry Spence had photographed really had belonged to her and her dead husband? She could hardly confront the man Susan Danner probably called Daddy and demand that his daughter's tissue be tested.

Meeting the child would probably be the strangest thing of all. Despite the distinct family resemblance, the face that looked up at her from the grainy print—impish, vulnerable, a bit strong-willed—was that of a stranger. If she *was* Margo's, except for the nine months of her gestation and the actual process of birth, they had no history together.

"Do you have an address?" she asked.

Harry Spence scribbled something on a piece of paper and handed it to her. His expression clearly stated that, while he disapproved of surveillance or any other facet of detective work being conducted by unlicensed individuals, it was entirely her own affair what she chose to do with it.

Not to be swayed, Margo folded the slip of paper and put it in her purse. "Were you able to find out anything at the hospital that might lead you to believe a switch actually occurred?" she asked.

The detective shook his head. "The records appeared to be in order, Mrs. Rourke. I'm sorry."

With a sigh, Margo got out her checkbook. "How much do I owe you?"

As she wrote out the stated fee, a strong desire to confirm or disprove the possibility that Susan Danner might be her baby drew up battle lines against the reluctance in her heart.

Margo had left the back door unlocked. Entering her Ravenna area craftsman-style bungalow through the kitchen door as she usually did, Nell found her sitting in a darkened living room. Perhaps because Nell dealt with distraught people every day, she knew better than to switch on a lamp.

"For heaven's sake, hon," she exclaimed, plunking herself down on the sofa and putting one arm about Margo's shoulders. "What's wrong? It's not like you to mope around this way."

There was a small silence. "I saw the detective this afternoon," Margo admitted at last.

Nell rolled her eyes. "Oh, geez. I forgot."

The two of them sat there for a moment, not saying anything further. Then Nell asked, "Have you eaten?"

Margo shook her head.

"Let me fix you something."

"I'm not very hungry."

"Well, *I* am." Giving her a squeeze, Nell took off her raincoat and strode back into the kitchen. Additional light seeped into Margo's sanctuary via the dining room. Before long the aroma of tomato soup and toasted cheese sandwiches filled the air.

It turned out that Margo was hungry after all. "I don't know what I'd do without you, Nell," she maintained as they settled at the small table in the breakfast nook.

Grayer than she'd been when Beth Ann was born but still pink-cheeked and hearty, Nell beamed. A naturally caring person, she'd been Margo's staunchest ally during crisis after crisis with Jim, and had fussed over Beth Ann as if the child had been her own granddaughter. "That goes double," she replied.

"You have Bert."

"Yeah, well. He's okay, I guess." Long divorced, Nell "kept company" with a local widower. But to date she hadn't expressed much interest in marrying him. "Want to tell me what the detective said?" she asked.

By now Margo was ready to talk. Quickly she outlined the essentials of her meeting with Harry Spence, including Seth Danner's advertisement for a housekeeper.

"I'm not sure what I want to do about it," she confessed with the soul weariness of someone who'd already wrestled with the problem for hours. "I know it's probably ill-advised, and might result in heartbreak. But I'm thinking of calling him..."

Nell was suddenly very quiet. "Sure you want to do that?" she asked skeptically.

"Surely you can understand that I have to *see* her...for Jim's sake as well as my own."

Nell's softening expression acknowledged that she did. "And if you think she's your daughter?" she prodded. "Or aren't sure? What then?"

"I might take the position if it's offered to me. It wouldn't have to be forever...just a couple of months."

"You'd actually give up your desktop publishing business to keep house for someone, now that you're doing so well?"

Margo shrugged. "In my line of work, you tend to have as much or as little business as you're willing to go after. I could cut back. Turn out the essential stuff on weekends. But that isn't the point, is it? You think I should let sleeping dogs lie. That I'd be making a big mistake."

Nell was silent for a moment. "Not a mistake, hon," she said at last. "More like a step into shark-filled waters. If you decide to take it, there'll be great risk attached, as well as a great potential reward. That's not me talking. It's the stars."

As usual, sensing Margo was at a crossroads, Nell had cast her horoscope. Margo wanted to be irritated. But she wasn't. She felt curiosity. And a certain uneasy fascination.

"Do the stars have any advice to offer?" she challenged, attempting to treat the whole thing as a joke.

Nell didn't laugh. "Just to tread carefully," she replied. "There are three lives at stake here... four, if you count the girl's mother's. But you don't need an astrologer to tell you that."

Margo sighed. Nell was right, of course. The action she was contemplating really did involve a big emotional risk for everyone concerned.

"I plan to be careful," she reassured her friend. "Don't think I haven't agonized over this. But I have to check on her, don't you see? Even if the whole thing's true and she *is* my daughter, I might never seek custody, or breathe a word of it to anyone. I just have to find out if she's happy, well cared for, and..." She paused, struggling for control. "I want to make sure...that she's truly loved."

Seth Danner had a nice telephone voice—warm, deep and resonant. He sounded like a big, thoroughly masculine man, with a well-developed sense of who he was and what he was doing in the world. As a yacht builder, Margo guessed, he'd be casual, muscular and outdoorsy. She sensed vitality and drive, a determination to master circumstances rather than let them master him.

"Can you tell me a little bit about your background, Mrs. Rourke?" he asked. "For instance, have you worked in this capacity before? Particularly where there's a child concerned?"

Usually quite adept at ad-libbing, Margo found she wasn't sure what to say. "I...yes," she answered. "That is, not exactly. But..."

The wariness Seth Danner had acquired in dealing with his parade of housekeepers quickly became evident. "Mind explaining yourself?" he inquired, polite but terse.

Truth was definitely called for. Or the interview would be over. "I'm a widow," she replied. "My only child, a daughter, died last year. I'm very good at caring for a home and looking after a little girl. It's just that I haven't done it for a salary before."

If it occurred to him that she might be trying to fill a void in her own life by seeking employment with him, he didn't say so. Nor did he give her any other clue to his thoughts. Instead, he excused himself for a moment to instruct someone about how he wanted something done. He was patient but definitive—clearly the boss of his operation.

Apparently something in her words had hit a positive note. "I'd really like to find someone as quickly as possible, Mrs. Rourke," he said, coming back on the line. "I'm interviewing at the boat yard. That's Danner Yachts, Inc. We're situated on the north shore of Lake Union, at the foot of the Aurora Avenue overpass. Could you come by tomorrow? Or, better still, this afternoon? With the names of several references?''

It was now or never. Margo decided to take the plunge. ''Actually, this afternoon would be convenient,'' she said.

For the interview, Margo dressed conservatively in a heather-gray turtleneck, matching slim wool skirt and flat shoes that added nothing to her five foot three inch height. But she couldn't seem to stifle the flamboyant side of her nature altogether. Unaware of the pizzazz they created, she fastened on a chunky gold necklace and topped her somber outfit with a swingy, bright gold, three-quarter-length wool coat that made a splash of color against the chilly, rain-soaked gloom.

As she parked her vintage M.G. Midget in the cindered lot outside Danner Yachts, Inc., a steady stream of cars, trucks and giant sixteen-wheelers roared across the soaring overpass. The lake was unpolished pewter, stippled by rain. Beyond the boatworks' roof, a forest of slender, white masts pierced the drizzle, swaying gently. In the distance a tug's horn bleated mournfully.

Not stopping to open her umbrella because she didn't want to risk having the time to pause and reflect, Margo ran the short distance from her parking space to a low annex marked Office. The reception area featured threadbare carpet, framed photographs of yachts and a cheerful pot of rust-colored mums.

''May I help you?'' a secretary asked.

Margo swallowed. ''I'm here to see Seth Danner.''

The woman gave her a friendly smile just as the phone started to ring. ''He's in the finishing shed...through that door and down the stairs,'' she said, reaching for the receiver. "There are cables all over the place . . . don't forget to watch your step!"

A bit apprehensively, Margo went in search of the man who might be raising her child. As she descended the rickety staircase, she couldn't help staring at the cavernous, unfamiliar surroundings in which she found herself. The boatworks was vast, much larger than she'd expected. Its high, corrugated fiberglass roof, which admitted a filtered, grayish light, began to ping gently when the rain came down a little harder.

At one end, huge doors opened to the marine ways, where some men were testing a medium-sized yacht with gasoline engines. Margo's nostrils flared at the mingled scents of motor oil, paint fumes and solvent. Somewhere a generator chugged steadily. Sanders whined in counterpoint to the creaking of an overhead crane's massive winches and the voices of men calling back and forth as they worked.

A laborer of about twenty or so, with a purple cap and spray paint on his dungarees, directed her to the finishing shed. Bulking in its slip was a large yacht in the final stages of completion. Margo guessed it to be at least sixty-five feet in length.

She didn't notice the tall, redheaded man in jeans and a nubby gray sweater right away. But he noticed her.

Who's that? Seth wondered, with more than casual interest. Not your typical yacht customer, that's for sure. I'll bet she's lost. She was just the sort of woman who appealed to him, though: slender, on the petite side, with a halo of naturally curly dark hair that had contracted to ringlets from all the humidity. He watched her closely; her movements were like quicksilver.

As Margo reached the finishing shed's lower level, a phone rang. One of the workers answered it. "Mrs. Rourke is here for her appointment," she shouted out.

Seth felt a lurch of surprise. It was quickly followed by the odd sense that somehow their meeting had been pre-destined. A fairly logical man, he decided he must be losing his grip.

"I'm Seth Danner," he announced, stepping forward to meet her. "Thanks for coming over."

He was about six foot two, and he had blond eye-brows. His tousled red-gold hair looked as if it had been raked back carelessly from his forehead. The sights, sounds and aromas of the shed seemed to recede as he held out one big, neatly manicured hand and Margo took it. I *know* him from somewhere, she thought as she gazed up at his broad shoulders and ruggedly handsome fea-tures. She could almost feel the vibrations of some past meeting connecting them.

Her fingers felt delicate wrapped in his. "Nice meet-ing you," she said.

For a moment, they just continued to look at each other.

"Let's go back upstairs to my office," Seth suggested, breaking the silence. "You'll be more comfortable there."

Seth's office had the same worn carpet as the recep-tion area and a big, comfortable looking desk littered with blueprints and paperwork. Standing a little too close for comfort, he offered to take her coat.

Reluctantly, because she didn't expect to be staying long, she shrugged it off, revealing a slim but shapely figure. Probably the best policy would be to forge straight ahead—get things over with as quickly as possible. She extracted several sheets of paper from a waterproof portfolio.

"The bottom sheet lists my references," she explained, perching on a high wooden stool in lieu of the only guest chair his working space provided.

The choice of seating emphasized her pretty legs. Yikes, thought Seth, trying not to stare at them as he took cover in his usual spot. *She's much younger than the sort of woman I envisioned. If I hire* her, *the neighbors will have a field day.* Yet he felt inexorably drawn to the warmth that sparkled in her lively dark eyes. He and Sooz desperately needed some of that.

"You'll note they stem from my work in public relations at Bayless Memorial eight years ago," she was saying.

"The references?"

"Yes. Since leaving there, I've worked out of my home, designing brochures and publications...that kind of thing."

He was definitely interested in her. "Why the contemplated switch to housework?" he asked, unconsciously turning on his heart-stopping smile.

Though she'd barely glanced at another man since Jim's death eight years earlier, Margo realized to her consternation that she wasn't immune. *He was gorgeous—like some big, tawny king of the jungle with that coppery-gold hair, those topaz eyes. In addition, he* felt *solid. Eminently trustworthy. I wonder if he has a temper?* she speculated with sudden insight. *Something tells me he can be pretty awesome when he's riled.*

Under the circumstances, she couldn't afford to get all moony over him. "I guess you could say I need a change," she responded. "Having people around, especially since my daughter's death. I miss her...very much."

Though she tried to maintain control, he caught the slight quiver of her lower lip. It brought out his protective instincts. Losing a child had obviously been hell for her. As a father who doted on his own charmingly problematical little girl, he could only imagine how terrible her grief must have been. If she could cook, and she was reliable...

"You say you've worked out of your home for the past eight years," he observed, striving to be practical. "Does that mean you own your own house here in the city? The person I hire must be willing to live in five days a week, from Sunday evenings through Friday afternoons. Would that present a problem?"

No doubt he'd had a steady stream of girlfriends since his divorce, as well as a parade of housekeepers, and wanted a built-in baby-sitter. A man who looked like that wouldn't find it difficult to avail himself of female companionship.

So what? Margo thought in annoyance. *You* won't be dating him. She shrugged. "I don't see why it should, provided my weekends were my own."

"Of course, you'd have your own room and bath, as well. You could decorate them any way you wished."

Though she nodded, she didn't comment.

"What about salary?" he continued, naming a figure. "Would it be sufficient to meet your needs? For instance, would it cover your mortgage payments?"

In Margo's opinion, the wages he was offering were more than generous. But she knew what he was driving at. The cost of housing in Seattle had skyrocketed during the past several years with an influx of buyers from

California. If she couldn't make ends meet, she wouldn't stay; and he'd be looking for a housekeeper again.

"I don't have a mortgage," she told him. "My late husband and I bought the property in 1981. His life insurance paid off the balance we owed. I just have to worry about taxes, which admittedly have jumped. In answer to your underlying question, I can afford to take the job."

Glancing at the cut of her clothing, which was simple but elegant and probably expensive, he decided she probably could. Yet she didn't seem to need it. Why was she giving his offer serious consideration?

"Sure it's the sort of thing you'd enjoy?" he persisted. "I'd like to find someone competent and reliable who'd feel comfortable, even fulfilled in the position, and wouldn't leave us after a month or so."

For the first time Margo wondered if Susan Danner was a brat. Maybe Nell was right. She *should* have thought things through with more deliberation before phoning for an interview. Well, that was a moot point now. She was *there,* in his office. I hate to waste his time, she thought, or deceive him, but I've got to get a look at her.

"If I agreed to take the position, I'd stay for at least six months," she volunteered. "But before I could make that kind of commitment, I'd have to see your home. And meet your daughter. Could you tell me a little about her?"

Seth was well aware that she'd turned the tables and had begun interviewing him. But she'd done it so forthrightly and gracefully he felt as if he were being stroked. "I have a picture of her right here," he said, picking up a brass-framed portrait from his desk and handing it to her.

The girl in the photograph resembled Margo's whimsical eight-year-old self even more than she had in the grainy black-and-white shot Harry Spence had taken. So? Margo thought. It's hardly conclusive evidence. People always insisted Beth Ann looked like me, too.

No matter how much you loved her, Beth wasn't your biological child, she reminded herself brutally. The tests proved that. You have to accept it, even if it hurts. Meanwhile, *this* girl might be yours. Would she be able to tell if they met in person? she wondered. Or was she kidding herself? Abruptly, she realized she was staring.

"She's very pretty," she said, glancing up into warm hazel eyes lit by tawny specks that resembled a sprinkling of gold dust trapped in amber.

He smiled that remarkable smile again, clearly susceptible to flattery when it focused on his child. "Naturally *I* think so," he answered. "But then, I'm biased. I might as well admit it up front...she can be a handful at times. Her mother and I were divorced a year and a half ago and she hasn't taken it very well. Sometimes I think she blames me. Yet we continue to be very close. I'm afraid I spoil her. I will say she responds to attention. Honesty. And lots of love."

He might not realize it, but he was asking Margo to care about his little girl—the selfsame sprite who might turn out to be her daughter instead of his. She could almost feel the sharks Nell had mentioned swimming around her ankles.

She placed the framed picture back on his desk with deliberate care. If she was going to finish what she'd started, she'd have to be tough. And steadfast. The alternative was to spend a lifetime wondering.

"When can I meet her?" she asked.

"Would you have time now? It's already past four-thirty. I'm not likely to get much more work done here today."

They were standing very close now, so close Seth could inhale her lily of the valley perfume. In his opinion, the fresh, delicate scent suited her perfectly. Was it possible this will-o'-the-wisp, pixieish female would be content to cook their meals and wash their dirty laundry? He felt like a cad asking her to perform such mundane tasks. Yet, incredibly, she seemed interested.

"We live in the Magnolia area," he added. "I'd be happy to drive you there. Or..."

Meeting Susan was why Margo had come. In the process of accomplishing that, though, she had to admit she wouldn't mind spending a little more time with Seth Danner. He had a lot of personal warmth and appeal.

"I suppose I could go over for a few minutes," she said, firmly quelling doubt and reservation. "I know the Magnolia section fairly well. If you'll give me your address, I'll follow you in my car."

It was November. Rush hour, and early dusk. The drizzle continued unabated. Consequently, traffic was heavy as Margo followed Seth's honey-tan Mercedes across the Fremont Bridge and around Queen Anne Hill to West Garfield Street. As she followed his distinctively patterned taillights, she was overcome with guilt. Put it any way you like, she thought, I *am* taking advantage of him.

He'd be furious if and when she ever had to tell him the truth. Yet, if she'd approached him at the outset with her mind-boggling suspicions, she felt certain Susan Danner would have been placed off limits to her immediately. If the girl was hers, she deserved a look.

Seth swung around to the left when they reached the intersection of Cliff and Magnolia. His home—gray-shingled and ultra-modern with black metal decking—turned out to be one of the favored few, with an unimpeded view of Puget Sound and the sparkle of downtown skyscrapers from a cliffside, waterfront setting. Its color blended into the twilight, misty and appropriate.

"You'll have to excuse the decor," he warned, getting out of the Mercedes. "It's post-divorce. Whatever my ex-wife *didn't* want, plus some pretty basic, utilitarian purchases I've made since. I'm not much of a decorator."

The foyer and large living room, with its stone fireplace and breathtaking wall of windows, were furnished mostly in gray and eggplant. Though the setting was fabulous, there were few homey touches.

"Sooz?" Seth Danner called out, doffing his raincoat. "Baby, I'm home."

"Daddy!"

Seconds later, he was enveloped by slender, little-girl arms. Margo watched with a lump in her throat. Susan and Beth had shared the same birthday. But by now, the child Seth had raised was almost two years older.

Wriggling free, Susan gazed up at her father. "Jill's mom and dad are taking her to the movies and they said I could come if it was all right with you," she announced in a somewhat wheedling tone. "They're leaving in fifteen minutes so they can catch the early show. Can I? Please! I already did most of my homework!"

Like a lion playing affectionately with its cub, Seth ruffled her curly dark hair. "What about the rest of it?" he asked. "And supper? You can't live on candy bars and popcorn, you know."

"Mrs. Johnson could make me a peanut butter and jelly sandwich before she goes."

Seth gave a helpless shrug. He seemed to be no match for Susan's wiles as long as she deferred to his basic rules. "There's somebody I'd like you to meet," he said.

For the first time, Susan glanced in Margo's direction. Her keen, dark eyes took on an expression of instant hostility. "Who are *you?*" she demanded bluntly. "Another one of Daddy's girlfriends, I suppose?"

Chapter Two

Could this unfriendly moppet actually be her child? The abrupt frontal attack only strengthened Margo's resolve to find out. With effort, she managed to keep her disapproval under wraps. At the moment, she guessed, the better part of valor would be to keep a low profile.

Seth was both embarrassed and annoyed on her behalf. "For heaven's sake, Sooz!" he exclaimed, a paternal frown drawing his blond brows together. "What kind of welcome is that? Mrs. Rourke isn't my girlfriend. But she might turn out to be our new housekeeper if you haven't already driven her from our door!"

Sooz, as her father called her, seemed anything but contrite. "We don't *need* a housekeeper, Daddy," she reasoned, like some pint-sized attorney warming to her case. "Mrs. Johnson takes care of me after school. And I look after you. I like things just the way they are!"

Seth and Margo glanced at each other. "Please...give us a chance," his beautiful eyes seemed to say. Just then, a gray-haired woman who was probably in her early seventies poked her head into the living room.

"I hate to interrupt, Mr. Danner," she said, clearly oblivious to her bad timing. "But I was wondering... will you be able to take me home now? Or should I call a cab?"

Margo's M.G. was parked behind Seth's Mercedes in the drive. If he had to take the baby-sitter home, it was going to require a bit of a shuffle. But that wasn't what caught Margo's attention. Thoughtfully, she considered the fact that she'd be left alone with Susan until his return. She found the prospect daunting yet rife with possibilities. What would they talk about? It was difficult to take her eyes off the girl's dusting of freckles, which reminded her of Jim's. The shape of her jaw was also reminiscent of his.

But apparently Seth wasn't ready to abandon her to his daughter's slings and arrows just yet. "If you don't mind, a cab would be preferable," he told Mrs. Johnson as he reached for his wallet. "I'll be happy to pay for it."

Accepting the money plus her daily fee with thanks, the baby-sitter retreated to the kitchen, where she could be heard dialing a phone.

"Now then," Seth told his daughter. "I think you should apologize to our guest."

Though his tone was kindly, there wasn't much doubt that he meant business. Sooz seemed to realize it at once, and responded. She turned to Margo with what seemed like real concern.

"I'm really sorry if I hurt your feelings," she said. "I didn't mean to. Honest. It's just..."

"That'll do." Seth gave the girl's hand a reassuring squeeze, which also served to silence any further explaining that might veer off in the wrong direction. "What do you say we show Mrs. Rourke around?"

Suddenly Sooz was all cooperation. "Of course, Daddy. But could we please hurry? And can I call Jill first? If we're going to the movies..."

Seth had decided not to relax the rules. However, he'd learned it was easier to deal with situations like this one if he negotiated a settlement.

"I'm afraid that won't be possible tonight, sweetheart," he said with genuine regret. "You know our agreement... homework and an early bedtime on school nights. I have an idea... why don't the two of us go tomorrow night instead? On Fridays, you can afford to stay up late. I'll take you out for pizza first."

Sooz's eyes lit up. "Super, Daddy! It's a date!"

Mollified, she skipped off to the kitchen to press chocolate-chip cookies on Mrs. Johnson, who was rustling about, getting her things together. Seconds later, Sooz could be heard chatting on the phone with her friend. She seemed to have forgotten her father's request that she help him give Margo the grand tour.

Maybe I'm riding for a fall once the truth sets in, Margo thought, but she didn't feel particularly maternal toward Sooz. At first blush, the child who might well be her flesh and blood—as well as Jim's—came off second-best in any comparison with Beth Ann. Though she seemed to possess twice Beth's energy and drive, Sooz certainly didn't share her counterpart's angelic nature. Still, there was something inherently likable, almost touching, about Sooz, despite her prickly outspokenness.

"I warned you," Seth reminded with a grin, throwing up his hands. "She can be quite a little gremlin sometimes. C'mon... I'll show you the quarters that'll be your private turf if we can reach an agreement, as well as the basic layout. The house has three stories, including an exposed basement. And, in case you haven't noticed, some pretty spectacular views."

The rooms Margo would call her own, if she decided to take on the challenge of keeping house for Seth Danner and his daughter, were pleasant indeed. In addition to a generously sized bedroom and bath, there was a small sitting room with a panoramic view of the Sound. As in the rest of the house, the furnishings were modern, bland and rather basic. But they seemed comfortable enough. With a few plants and pillows to brighten things up...

Margo hauled herself up short as Seth offered glimpses of Sooz's room—messy, with a stuffed teddy bear in the place of honor on her bed—and his own—masculine and lacking in personality, with blond oak furniture. Watch it, she reminded herself. Your purpose here is to check out a child who, through some trick of fate, might be yours from a biological standpoint. Beyond that, you don't have any legitimate business, or commitment.

As they headed downstairs, she reflected that at least the question of love had been resolved to her satisfaction. Seth Danner might be a single parent struggling to provide the kind of upbringing a mother and father acting in concert could have managed with more finesse, but he plainly showered the girl he'd nicknamed Sooz with affection. Despite any lingering unhappiness over her parents' divorce, she seemed relatively secure.

The basement contained laundry facilities, a storage area and a large recreation room that also had a stunning view. By the time they returned to the well-equipped but unremarkable kitchen, Sooz was off the phone, finishing her homework at the kitchen table and nibbling at the chocolate-chip cookies she and Mrs. Johnson had doubtless made together. And from the expression on Seth's face, Margo got the distinct impression that Sooz was violating a prohibition against spoiling her supper.

With a casual air, Seth opened the oven door and peered inside to see what the baby-sitter had left for their evening meal. "Tuna casserole," he mused, giving his daughter a sidelong glance. "I guess we're having it for dessert."

Sooz had the grace to look abashed.

A few minutes later Seth was walking Margo to her car. "Well? What do you think?" he asked, standing bare-headed in the drizzle as she rested her hand on the M.G.'s convertible top. "Sooz isn't always such a terror. At times, she can be rather sweet. Do you find the prospect of working for us just too much?"

Awash in conflicting emotions, Margo didn't answer him right away. Now that Sooz wasn't on the scene to distract her, she could feel the tug of Seth's masculinity a hundredfold. The man exerted a sensual pull on her like nothing she'd ever experienced. And she could ill afford the complication. Still, she knew she'd regret it if she never saw him again.

She also wanted to see more of Sooz.

"Does that question mean you're offering me the job?" she countered.

It was Seth's turn to appear thoughtful, but he'd already made up his mind. Pixie that she was, Margo Rourke hadn't allowed Sooz to bully her. Nor had she appeared to take the girl's bad manners personally, though she'd almost certainly disapproved of them. It was anybody's guess if she could cook or clean. But suddenly those skills seemed secondary. He had a strong feeling she possessed exactly the right bag of tricks needed to manage his daughter.

Regarding her from the eleven-inch disparity in their heights, Seth recalled Sooz's characterization of Margo as his "girlfriend." I wonder what would've happened if we'd met in some other way, he thought. It's a foregone conclusion that I'd have asked her for a date. And I have a feeling it wouldn't have ended there. Yet if she agreed to take the job, they'd have to keep things on a business footing.

Slowly but steadily, soft rain was soaking him to the skin and depositing tiny, jewellike beads of moisture on Margo's lashes. As she gazed up at him, they were clumped together like the points of stars. Her mist-drenched hair was as curly as a gypsy's, a sensuous tangle about her face.

With difficulty, Seth kept his hands to himself. She was waiting for an answer.

"It seems that I am," he acknowledged at last. "But I don't expect you to give me your answer right away. Maybe you could think things over tonight and call me at my office . . . say tomorrow afternoon?"

Though Margo fully intended to spend the evening at her computer catching up on missed work, she found it impossible to concentrate. You'd be insane to move in with Seth Danner and go to work as his housekeeper, she thought, pushing her chair back from the desk and heading upstairs to run herself a bubble bath. The job's far beneath your capabilities. Yet if she told him no, it was doubtful she'd see him or his daughter again.

And she wanted to. She had to admit that much.

You won't learn anything more by cooking his meals and washing his windows, she reminded herself as she poured out a glass of wine, lit a candle and sank down into the suds. You'll just grow fond of the child despite her bratty ways. And maybe of him. The only way you'll ever get a concrete answer is to talk him into submitting her for a tissue test.

But, after meeting Seth, she guessed she didn't have a snowball's chance in hell of convincing him to do that. She couldn't even think of a way to broach the subject. Though he seemed the most amiable of men when things were going his way, her intuition told her he was more than capable of a blowup. He was a redhead, wasn't he? And he'd have every reason to be angry if he ever learned what her real purpose had been in contacting him. God knows she'd feel the same if the situations were reversed.

What on earth was she going to do? She'd promised him an answer. And the moment of truth was less than twenty-four hours away. As rain fell softly against her windowpane, Margo soaked and pondered.

Seth had given up hope of hearing from her by the time the phone rang in his office at 5:02 p.m. the following afternoon. Already half into his raincoat, he reached for the receiver.

"Mrs. Rourke on one," Josie informed him in a tone that indicated she was on her way out the door.

He could barely control his relief, or the surge of eagerness he felt as he pressed the flashing red button on his console. "Hi," he said. "I'm glad you caught me. After the way Sooz behaved yesterday, I'd all but decided you wouldn't phone."

"Was there ever any doubt?"

There was a smile in her voice. His hopes shot up a notch or two, revealing just how much he'd been counting on her acceptance. Something told him that if Margo Rourke came to live with them, they wouldn't be looking for a replacement in six months. What was more, the dramatic but somehow lifeless house where he and his little girl rattled around together would become a home.

Hell, he thought, trying not to jinx things. She's probably going to let me down easy. And I wouldn't blame her. We're not the plummiest of prospects.

"So," he said, taking the initiative. "Do I dare ask what you've decided?"

Though the decision had been a tough one, Margo didn't hesitate. "If you like, I can start on Monday," she answered. "At the agreed upon salary. And with the six-month proviso I mentioned. I believe we discussed the fact that I won't be available on weekends. I'll be spending them at my place."

Seth was stunned. She was really going to do it! He wanted to jump for joy. If she'd been present in his office, he'd have waltzed her around the room. I've got to have a serious talk with Sooz, he thought. This time, she can't be allowed to screw things up.

"Mr. Danner?" Margo prompted. "Are you still there?"

"I'm here. Please...call me Seth. I guess you could say I'm bowled over. And very pleased. I noticed your car is about as small as they get. Can I help you move anything? A television and linens are provided, of course. But you may want to bring some of your own things to make the place more habitable..."

He realized that, in his excitement, he was rambling.

"Thanks, I would like to bring a few things from home," she answered. "But you don't need to worry about hauling them. I have access to a station wagon. If you'll leave a key under the mat, I'll let myself in Monday morning . . . after Sooz has left for school."

Seth agreed her plan was probably best. With her strong territorial instincts, Sooz might prove a sullen onlooker were Margo to move in while she was present. But if Margo appeared firmly entrenched, already a fixture of the household on his daughter's arrival from school, it might serve to ease their initial confrontation. For his part, he was definitely looking forward to having a dark-eyed angel of mercy under his roof.

"Sounds fine to me," he assured her. "Again, I can't tell you how happy this makes me."

If you only knew what my reasons were, Margo thought guiltily, you wouldn't feel that way. The truth was, she liked Seth a lot more than was advantageous for either of them. She hated deceiving him.

"Well, see you Monday," she said as casually as she could. "Feel free to phone me in the meantime if you think of anything. Enjoy your movie tonight."

Stopping by to pick up Margo for a planned evening out, Nell had arrived in time to catch the last half of her conversation. "So you're actually going through with it," she observed after Margo and Seth had said goodbye.

Margo nodded. "I'd never forgive myself if I didn't. Sooz Danner may be 'quite a handful,' as her father puts it, but she might also be my daughter. I need to know her a whole lot better before I decide whether or not to reveal the set of circumstances that led me to her door, or relinquish any claim I might have to her."

She couldn't bring herself to confess that her attraction to Seth Danner had also been a significant factor in her decision-making.

Clearly aware more was going on than met the eye, Nell regarded her with a questioning expression. "There's something different about you," she remarked at last. "Something that can't be attributed to meeting this child. I should have taken a look at your chart."

Though she didn't enlighten her friend, Margo knew just what that something was. For the first time since Jim's death, she felt like a living, breathing woman—one with sensual desires. And needs. A man who towered over her like a giant oak, with red-gold hair and eyes like topaz, was responsible.

Since Nell followed the positions of the planets from day to day, maybe she'd plot a quick horoscope in her head and guess.

"C'mon," Margo urged, nudging her off the scent. "We might as well get going if you want to have a bite of supper before the concert starts."

Determined not to submerge her identity in the role of housekeeper, Margo borrowed Nell's station wagon to convey an assortment of books, pillows, plants and framed pictures to the Danner residence. She even brought over the hand-quilted bedspread and shams from the room that had once been Beth's.

Returning for her M.G., Margo left Nell's vehicle in her own regular parking space at home so her friend could pick it up after work. Though she clearly had misgivings about what Margo was doing, Nell was being supportive, as usual. She'd even arranged a ride with a friend so she could pick up her ancient Volvo without Margo having to be involved.

Returning to the house on Magnolia, Margo went to work on her personal space. Using special hooks that wouldn't damage the walls, she put up some of her favorite prints. Books she'd been planning to read lined an empty bookcase. Toss pillows and an afghan materialized on the couch in her sitting room. When she was finished, her quarters were the most attractive in the house.

There wasn't much time to whip up a spectacular meal, thanks to the move. The Danners would have to settle for an old-fashioned, everyday supper.

She was in the kitchen, putting the finishing touches to a meat loaf and a casserole of baked beans when Sooz walked in the door. The dark-haired sprite who looked so much like Margo's childhood self didn't speak as she headed first for the refrigerator and then to the cookie jar.

"Hi, Sooz," Margo said, glancing up from her work but not making a big deal of it.

There wasn't any answer. Helping herself to a glass of orange juice and a handful of cookies, Sooz flopped down at the kitchen table and turned on the television set. Thoughtfully she munched and sipped, ignoring both Margo and the school books at her elbow.

"Don't you have homework tonight?" Margo asked.

In the blink of an eyelash, Sooz switched from seeming indifference to absolute fury and loathing. "You're not my parent! You can't tell me what to do!" she huffed. "Where's Mrs. Johnson? I'd rather have *her!*"

Margo shrugged. "Now that I'm here, she isn't needed. I asked you about your homework."

Sooz folded slender arms across her chest, telegraphing all the classic signs of resistance. "I don't want you here! I'm sick of housekeepers," she said. "All they ever do is boss me around. And leave, the minute I get used to them. I'd rather have Mrs. Johnson. At least she can cook."

Margo tried not to smile. "I guess you must hate meat loaf and baked beans," she commented, taking a boxed mix down from the cupboard. "Not to mention chocolate cake."

In answer, Sooz stuck out her tongue.

Seth came home with anticipation written all over his face. Once again, he was dressed in jeans and a sweater, as if he'd spent another day in the finishing shed. This time the sweater was gold, with a rolled collar. A little more form-fitting than the one he'd worn the day they'd met, it hinted at the well-developed muscles of his chest and upper arms. In Margo's opinion, jeans didn't have any right to fit a human body the way his did.

"Hi, sweetheart," he said, giving Sooz a squeeze, which she rewarded with a stingy peck. "Hello, Margo. Something sure smells terrific."

Somebody looks terrific, too, he thought, though he didn't dare say so. Trim and shapely in her forest green sweater and ivory corduroy trousers, with her hair curling from the heat of the oven, Margo was a vision of domesticity and sexiness. On her, an apron was almost as enchanting as a negligee.

The idea that both qualities could exist so harmoniously in one woman fired Seth's imagination. He suddenly wished her duties included giving him a welcome-home kiss.

"Meat loaf, baked beans and chocolate cake." She smiled. "Plus a salad. I'm glad you're hungry. Apparently I managed to pick everything Sooz detests."

Seth glanced at his daughter in surprise. "But that's nonsense," he averred. "Sooz loves meat loaf. Why, only last week . . ."

He paused as he caught Margo's wink. So Sooz had been giving her a hard time already. Well, he'd see about that!

Uh-uh, Margo signaled with a slight shake of her head. *Let me handle it. Everything will be all right.*

Wonder of wonders, Sooz hadn't terrorized her yet. It seemed he'd struck pay dirt. Excusing himself with what he suspected would be the first of many contented grins, Seth went upstairs to wash.

They ate in the dining area, in front of a window that spread the glitter of downtown and the muted sparkle of Alki Point at their feet. Though the meal was simple, Margo had lighted a couple of candles and arranged some yellow mums from her garden at home in an oversized mug for a centerpiece. Taking his place at the head of the table, Seth began to believe his beleaguered personal life was finally straightening out.

His sense of well-being notwithstanding, dinner was a somewhat uneven affair, with Sooz sulking and uncommunicative, though she was too hungry not to eat. He and Margo made the best of it, chatting amiably about books they'd read and upcoming events. Afterward he suggested Sooz help Margo with the dishes while he fixed the faucet in the laundry room.

"Why do I have to?" the girl protested at once, giving Margo a hostile look. "She's getting paid, isn't she?"

"*She* happens to have a name," Seth replied, in no mood to put up with his daughter's shenanigans. "It's *Mrs. Rourke.* I suggest you use it whenever you refer to 'her.' As for helping out, that's expected of everyone in this household. Understood?"

"Yes, *sir.*"

Obviously still rebellious, though she didn't dare go against her father's wishes, Sooz began clearing the table with the ferocity of a whirlwind.

Seth shook his head regretfully as she disappeared into the kitchen with a stack of plates and silverware. "Sorry about that display of temper," he apologized. "Unfortunately you might be treated to more of the same for a while. When Cheryl left—Cheryl's my ex-wife and Sooz's mother—Sooz was devastated. I'm afraid I spoiled her as a result. Now we're paying the price. I want you to know I'll back any reasonable disciplinary measures on your part. And that . . . well, I hope you'll hang in there."

Whenever she and Seth talked one-on-one, Margo felt as if they were the only two people in the world. He'd raised the girl who might be her daughter and, unable to stop herself, she imagined him as her husband. In her opinion, his ex-wife had been crazy to walk out on him.

Thank heaven her more sensible self remembered she wasn't in love with Seth. For one thing, she didn't know him well enough. And, for another, she couldn't afford to be. If she ever decided to pursue the subject of Sooz's parentage, they'd be on opposite sides of the fence. She'd just have to stop wishing he'd touch her every time they were together.

A rueful smile tilted the corners of her mouth. "Please don't feel as if I'm going to abandon you at any moment," she said. "Where Sooz is concerned, I've just begun to fight."

Chapter Three

Alone in her sitting room after packing Sooz's lunch, setting the coffeemaker to timed-brew and drawing up a marketing list, Margo finally realized what had been nagging at her since she'd first contacted Seth. She'd been concentrating on only half of the equation.

Genetic tests had proved Beth didn't belong, biologically, to her and Jim. It followed that, if Jim had been Sooz's dad and she was the girl's mother, then Seth had fathered the child she'd raised. With Sooz and Beth the only two female Caucasian infants in the Bayless Memorial nursery following their births, no other conclusion was possible.

In other words, Margo thought with a stirring of gooseflesh as she curled up beneath her afghan and listened to the rich chords of Ralph Vaughan Williams's "Theme from Thomas Tallis" play at low volume on her portable stereo, I've nursed his child at my breast. Kissed her good-night and wished her sweet dreams from her first day on this earth until she died in that accident.

It seemed she and Seth were connected by bonds that went far deeper than the schoolgirl crush she'd begun to develop for him.

As a result of her astrological studies, Nell had confided that she supported the theory of karma and reincarnation. It was her stated belief that people who were important to each other in past lives often reincarnated together. Supposing there was some basis in fact for those beliefs, Margo thought. Could experiences in another lifetime have drawn Seth and her together?

The idea was pretty farfetched from her point of view. But she had to admit it—Nell's astrological calculations and the inferences she'd drawn from them had proven amazingly accurate to date. Margo was eager to share her thoughts with her friend and ask a few questions. She wished it weren't too late to call.

Reaching for Beth Ann's picture, which she'd placed on a nearby table, Margo studied the elfin, heart-shaped face she loved so much. But, try as she might, she couldn't detect any resemblance between the dark-eyed child she'd lost and Seth with his hazel eyes and red-gold hair. In the past, she'd always believed Beth had inherited her coloring. I wonder what Cheryl's like, she thought now. Maybe she has dark hair and eyes, too.

She glanced up at a knock on her door.

"Margo...are you awake?" Seth called.

"Yes. Come in." Replacing Beth Ann's photograph, she reached for the stop button on her stereo.

Seth paused just inside the door. "Don't turn it off. That's a lovely piece of music."

"I'll just lower the volume so we can talk."

Seth glanced around the transformed sitting room. "I can't believe this is the same place I showed you just a few days ago," he said with a shake of his head. "With a little of this and that, you've made it very inviting. I wish you could work the same magic on the rest of the house."

Margo shrugged, embarrassed by the praise. She'd hardly done anything. Yet she knew what he meant. Beautiful as it was architecturally, his house was crying out for the personal touches that had given her quarters such a comfortable look.

"I suppose I could tackle it in my spare time, if you don't mind footing the bill," she offered. "You wouldn't need to spend a lot of money. You already have the basics. Besides, it's the little things that count."

What a contrast she is to Cheryl, Seth thought. A year and a half after his divorce, he was still paying off his ex-wife's credit card charges for, among other things, costly but somehow impersonal objets d'art that now graced his successor's million dollar Hawaii condominium. Meanwhile, orders at Danner Yachts, Inc., had fallen off, thanks to the 1991 federal luxury tax that had increased the price tag on the firm's top-of-the-line models by ten percent. He'd had to lay off a few people. And that had hurt.

Despite his financial concerns, though, he was still in the black, and he considered Margo's services a bargain. He believed that, in time, she'd bring Sooz around and establish peace and order in his home. The prospect was worth a great deal to him.

Before she'd walked into his life, he'd been convinced he'd never marry again. Now he wasn't so sure. Though Sooz seemed to hate every unattached woman he introduced, an inner voice kept whispering it was too bad he and Margo hadn't met in some other way. If they had, he

most certainly would have romanced her—maybe even
offered her a more intimate and permanent place in his
life, provided she and his daughter could manage to get
along. But now that she was his employee, he didn't feel
comfortable making romantic overtures.

With a start, he realized she was studying him.

"Won't you sit down?" she asked. "That little rocker
doesn't look as if it would hold you, but you're welcome
to the opposite end of the couch."

Seth wished he felt free to accept—her smile, her
warmth, were getting to him—but he couldn't.

"No, thanks," he said. "It's getting late. I just wanted
to tell you again how much I appreciate your taking this
job, despite its obvious drawbacks. And to say you
needn't spend your evenings cooped up in here if you'd
rather not. I want you to feel like part of the family. As
far as I'm concerned, you have the run of the house."

For Margo the next few days were hectic as she orga-
nized the Danner household and established a routine.
She didn't have time to phone Nell right away.

Bit by bit, Sooz's overt hostility faded; perhaps she'd
concluded it wasn't having much effect. In any case, Seth
had left her with little doubt. He wasn't prepared to stand
for it. Yet Margo knew the battle hadn't been won by any
means. Sooz's refusal to accept her had just gone under-
ground, to manifest itself in more subtle ways. On one
occasion, she'd "accidentally" slopped chili all over the
range top, creating a burned-on, sticky mess. And one of
her favorite tricks was pretending not to hear when
Margo asked her a question.

More stubborn than she'd realized she had the power
to be, Margo refused to let the girl provoke her into an
argument. Instead she repeated herself a lot, calling on

every shred of patience she possessed. When Sooz made a mess, she simply handed her the cleanser. Or a broom. Stubborn hearts aren't won over in a day, she told herself firmly. It'll take time to make friends with her. In the meantime, she'd keep a low profile. And wait.

That week Danner Yachts received a lucrative rush order. With Margo in command of the home front, Seth felt free to put in extra time at work. On Thursday he barely made it home in time to kiss Sooz good-night. Afterward, he hung around in the kitchen, chatting with Margo as she reheated his supper, then asked her to keep him company while he ate it at the coffee table in the living room in front of a crackling fire. The feeling was incredibly cozy, as if he'd been coming home to her for years.

Her every logical thought and instinct crying out that he was Beth's father, she found it easy to imagine Seth as her husband. You can't let yourself think of him that way, she warned herself. He'd be outraged if he knew your reason for being here. Since you might have to tell him the truth someday, getting emotionally involved with him would be a big mistake.

Yet she couldn't help the spontaneous attraction she felt. Or keep from wondering if it was reciprocated. She wanted to melt every time she looked into tawny eyes shaded by impossibly boyish, straw-colored lashes, and felt the strong physical tug of his presence.

Friday was Nell's day off. Margo had planned to have dinner downtown with her and do a little shopping after Seth returned home from work and she was free to leave. Around eleven o'clock Friday morning, with the initial backlog of housework out of the way, Margo dialed her friend's number.

"Hi . . . can I ask a favor?" she blurted out when Nell came on the line.

As usual, Nell was more than willing to help.

"If the genetic tests and Harry Spence's report are accurate, my new employer was probably Beth Ann's biological father, while I'm Sooz's mother," Margo explained. "Since I might find myself broaching a very delicate topic to him one of these days, I want to know everything I can about the type of man he is. And how to deal with him. I was wondering . . ."

Nell didn't have to be hit over the head with a two-by-four to guess what her friend had in mind. "You want me to do his chart," she stated.

"Umm, yes. I'd appreciate it. What kind of details do you need?"

If Nell was surprised by Margo's sudden enthusiasm for astrology as a decision-making tool, she didn't say so. "Just the basics," she replied. "Date of birth. And the exact time, if possible. Without that, we won't be able to project his rising sign."

Margo didn't have either fact at her fingertips, but she was determined to lay hold of both. "I'll have to find out and let you know," she said. "In the meantime, we do have Sooz's time of birth, thanks to Mr. Spence. It was 9:45 a.m. And of course her birthday and Beth's were the same. If you could do her chart, too, I'd be very grateful."

"I'll get started on it right away. Anything *else* I can do for you?"

Margo laughed. She knew Nell's ostensibly pointed query was a joke. Just the same, she felt somewhat demanding, laying claim to part of Nell's day off that way. "Not at the moment," she murmured. "Naturally I'll be happy to reimburse you for your time and effort."

Nell could almost be heard to bristle. "Since when did I charge for a service that gives me so much pleasure, hon? You know I follow the stars for the sheer fascination of it. Besides, having a ringside seat at the magic lantern show that's unfolding in your life is reward enough. By the way..."

Briefly Margo's friend paused, as if choosing her words with care. "There's nothing in your chart that would prevent you from seeking the information we need in Seth Danner's personal files if you felt that course of action was justified," she added finally. "I wasn't sure if I ought to mention it."

Seth trusted Margo. He'd given her the run of the house. But she doubted he'd go along with her riffling his desk and the filing cabinet he kept in his den. Unfortunately Nell was right. Her scruples weren't strong enough to dissuade her from doing just that in what she considered to be a worthy cause.

I don't plan to use the information to hurt him in any way, she rationalized as she slid open his middle desk drawer and began her search. Or to pry into his personal business. Just to smooth the course of events.

She didn't find anything in the desk, except for the usual paper clips, stray pencils, ballpoint pen cartridges, bills, canceled checks and mailing envelopes. However, she got lucky when she started riffling through the top drawer of Seth's filing cabinet. He'd stashed a copy of his birth certificate in a folder marked Personal Papers, along with his divorce decree and several other documents. With her conscience squawking in protest, she was careful not to look at any of them.

Quickly, though at that hour she wasn't likely to be interrupted at the task, she took down the pertinent facts.

A native of Seattle, Seth had been born on August 9, 1954 at 1:25 a.m. That made him thirty-eight years old. And a Leo. From her limited knowledge of astrology, the designation fit. She just couldn't figure out why it rang such a clearly discernable chord in her head.

Nell was waiting for her in the sedate but elegant Frederick and Nelson Restaurant, which was situated on the eighth floor of the department store of the same name. She'd managed to secure a quiet, out-of-the-way table beside one of the potted palms. Though their view of the piano player was blocked by a square, mirrored column, they were right beside one of the sweeping windowed walls, that offered a sparkling evening panorama of the surrounding buildings.

Margo felt a little rush of excitement as they ordered and the waitress brought them each a glass of chablis. "Well?" she asked the moment they were alone, unable to contain herself. "Did you do Sooz's chart?"

Nell smiled. "I have it right here."

Reaching into her oversize handbag, Nell drew forth several photocopied diagrams of the zodiac, characterized by the familiar wheel motif. Two were filled in. One was blank. She handed one of the two annotated sheets across the table.

"That's a copy of Beth's," she said. "As you know, I did it some time ago. I brought it along tonight for comparison's sake. For starters, we know both girls were born on the same day. Both are Sagittarians. The key to the difference between Susan Danner's strong-willed character and Beth's gentler nature lies in their rising signs.

"Beth's was Libra. It tended to refine and soften her outlook. By contrast, Susan's is Capricorn. She's sentimental but prickly, the type who'll never forget but *can* forgive.

"As you probably know, those born under Sagittarius, the sign of the Archer, can be somewhat blunt. Well, get this . . . our little prize package has three other planetary influences in that sign—Jupiter, Uranus and Neptune! No wonder she's so fearfully honest and outspoken!"

Margo rolled her eyes. "Is there any hope?"

"Oh, definitely." Nell took a sip of her wine. "Her moon is in Virgo, making her a little insecure and secretly critical of herself. I suspect that, every time she hits you with one of her zingers, it hurts her twice as much."

Margo had guessed at Sooz's hidden vulnerability herself. As her first week in Seth Danner's employ had drawn to a close, she'd found herself wanting to hug the girl when she was being her most obstreperous.

"Go on," she said.

Nell grinned. "You're going to love this. With her Mars in Libra, which is represented by the scales of justice, Susan will fight to the death for her beliefs. Only by convincing her that your presence in the household is right will you persuade her to call a truce. With her Uranus in Sag, you'll have to do it with tact and delicacy. She probably wouldn't want anyone to second-guess her. Or have her pegged."

Just then the waitress brought their salads. Since neither of them had bothered with lunch, they munched contentedly in silence for several minutes. At last Nell put down her fork.

"What did your big, handsome redhead turn out to be?" she asked with obvious curiosity. "A Leo?"

Margo almost choked on a radish. "How did you know?"

"It stood to reason. When's his birthday?"

She dug in her purse for the answer. "August 9, 1954, at 1:25 a.m.," she said, reading from her hastily scrawled note.

Pulling the corresponding book of statistics out of her purse, Nell didn't open it for a moment.

"Generally speaking," she said, "Leo men are strong but gentle, even chivalrous...unless they're stroked the wrong way. Then you get sparks if not a roar of outrage, particularly if their dignity is hurt. Since our specimen is sixteen degrees Leo—right in the middle—that would be particularly true of him.

"Leo men enjoy being the boss. Even the quieter ones love to be the center of attention. If you want to win one over, be his audience. When they're accorded what they believe is their proper respect, they're very affectionate with their mates. And their cubs. Family is of utmost importance to them. They'll literally die without love."

Knowing Nell as she did, Margo suspected her friend's observations about love and the affectionate nature of Leo males constituted something of a fishing expedition. She didn't intend to bite.

Nell gave her an appraising look. "The typical Leo needs a capable, loving lioness to run his kingdom. If one isn't available at the moment, he'll look for—and find— the next best thing. In Seth Danner's case, he found *you* to be his housekeeper. As for his role in the tangled skein of events you're trying to unravel, you might be interested to know Leos are often separated in some way from their children. Now let's take a look at his natal chart."

Thumbing through her book, Nell found the correct page and studied it a moment. "Hmm," she said. "This is interesting. His Saturn is in Scorpio, the same as Susan's. They'd have a strong karmic connection, even if he weren't her real dad.

"And another thing, your rising sign is Scorpio. The two of you probably have a powerful karmic connection, as well. You're apt to feel guilty if you try to keep secrets from him." Nell paused. "I wouldn't be surprised if there's a strong physical attraction between you..."

Margo could feel herself blushing. "I have to admit he's quite a hunk," she conceded. "But you know the situation's an impossible one."

Nell didn't agree or disagree with her statement. "His rising sign is Taurus," she continued, "which gives him added strength. And Leos are pretty strong to begin with! Since it's opposite your Scorpio, and his moon, Sagittarius, is opposite Gemini, your sun, the attraction I spoke of a moment ago is further enhanced. Taurus rising tends to make him a very sensual man. He probably has women falling all over him."

So far, Margo hadn't seen any sign of the harem she'd expected. And to be honest, she didn't want to. She pressed her wineglass against one burning cheek in an unconscious gesture.

Nell made some additional notations on Seth's chart. "I don't know if you're interested," she remarked, "but both his Venus and Neptune are in Libra. He's likely to be one heck of a lover. Plus, he's likely to be the sort of man who gets under a woman's skin. Leo men with planetary influences in Taurus and Libra are usually quite lovable in nature, you know, though they definitely have a temper. I trust you haven't seen anything of that yet."

Saved by the chicken pot pie, Margo thought with relief as their waitress deposited identical specialties of the house in front of them. "Actually, no," she reassured her friend. "So far, he's been more of a lamb than a lion."

Margo was removing a sheet of perfectly browned peanut-butter cookies from the oven Thursday afternoon when she caught sight of Sooz slipping into the house with a tear-stained face. I wonder what's wrong? she thought, wiping her hands on her apron. Has she skinned her knee or something? Without warning, the maternal feelings that had largely eluded her thus far crept into her heart.

Following the girl upstairs, she found Sooz's door firmly shut. "Sooz? Are you okay?" she asked.

There wasn't any answer.

Sooz would be nine in just two weeks. But that wasn't very old in the overall scheme of things. Deciding to butt in, Margo tapped lightly and opened the door.

"Go away!"

Sooz had flung her schoolbooks on the floor and flopped down on her stomach across the bed with one arm around her stuffed teddy. Every line of her body spelled misery.

"I will if you really want me to," Margo promised, "*after* you tell me what's wrong. If you're hurt, it's my job to apply disinfectant. And a bandage."

For some reason the bland, unemotional approach got through. "I'm fine," Sooz insisted, affording Margo a glimpse of her puffy, reddened face. "I got into trouble at school, that's all. And it wasn't my fault!"

"Want to tell me about it?"

"No! You're just the housekeeper here."

Margo stifled a flash of temper. Though Sooz had just shot her another barb, she thought she perceived an opening.

"Okay," she said, sitting down on the end of the bed. "I'll tell you about something that happened to me instead."

Sooz kept her back turned and her face hidden as Margo began to relate an episode that had taken place when she was in the second grade. But she didn't demand again that Margo leave the room.

"I put pepper in another girl's milk one day after she grabbed my cupcake," Margo recalled. "Of course, she told the teacher, and that teacher wasn't very nice. She did something a teacher should never, never do. Everyone who got in trouble that lunch hour had to take a turn wearing toy handcuffs. There were a lot of tears, I can tell you. It was very embarrassing for all of us."

Slowly Sooz turned over. "What did you do?" she asked, surprise and interest in her voice.

Margo pretended not to notice that Sooz was softening. "I was last in line," she said. "Watching the other kids bawl, I decided I wouldn't give that teacher—or the rest of the class—the satisfaction of seeing me do the same thing. When my turn came, I rested my chin on my hands and stared at the clock until my twenty minutes were up. Guess I'd make a pretty unrepentant jailbird, huh?"

By now, Sooz was sitting up, facing her. "So... you didn't cry at all?" she demanded, obviously wishing she could make a similar boast.

Margo wanted to hug her. She managed to restrain herself. "Ah, but I did," she admitted, "after I got home. When I told my dad about it, he laughed. It made me feel terrible."

"*My* dad wouldn't laugh," Sooz vowed, quick to seize an opportunity for one-upmanship. "He'd get mad at me if he thought I did something bad. But he wouldn't make fun of me."

"I don't think my dad meant it. That's just how he was. My mom fixed me hot chocolate. And that made me feel better."

Sooz was silent a moment. "Did you ever ask your dad why he laughed?" she asked finally. "I mean, after you were all grown up?"

Margo shook her head. "No, I never did. You see, he died the year after the handcuff incident, when I was your age. He and my mother were killed in a plane crash. So I never had the chance."

Sooz's eyes widened in pity. "Wow," she exclaimed in a hushed voice. "That must have been awful for you, losing both your parents! I have my dad. And I get to talk to my mother sometimes. She lives in Hawaii, you know."

"Yes, I did know that," Margo confessed. "Whatever happened today at school, I'm sure that, if it needs to be straightened out, your dad will take care of it. What would you say to washing your face and coming downstairs for a few peanut-butter cookies and some hot chocolate with marshmallows on top? We might be able to arrange a dispensation from homework until after supper."

When he walked in the door that night, Seth found phone-order pizza on the menu instead of lovingly prepared comfort food. But he didn't mind. To his amazement, Margo was seated at the kitchen table with Sooz, sketching the girl a set of homemade paper dolls. Clearly charmed by her creative ability, his prickly daughter was chattering away like a friendly monkey.

His amazement only deepened when Sooz mentioned her run-in at school—she'd pinched another girl who'd played keep-away with her lunch box—and retold the handcuff story that night at the dinner table. Had she and Margo progressed to the point of sharing confidences, then? Never in his wildest dreams had he expected the transition to friendship between them to be that easy.

When it was cleanup time, Margo gave Sooz an added break. "Go up and do your homework, babe," she said. "There aren't that many dishes. I can handle them by myself."

Always pleased to get out of chores, Sooz didn't have to be told twice. She ran lightheartedly up the stairs.

"You don't need to," Seth remarked in a husky voice, following Margo into the kitchen.

"Need to *what?*"

"Do the dishes by yourself. I'll be glad to help."

"Thanks. But it's really not necessary."

"I insist."

As usual, strong sensual vibrations crackled between them. Seth was looking down at her as if he planned to have her for dessert. It made Margo feel unsteady on her feet.

I'll bet Nell was right about his lovemaking ability, she thought, thoroughly smitten with him. He's probably like some great passionate archangel in bed.

Shivers swept over her when he leaned down to kiss her lightly on the cheek. "That's for being so good to Sooz," he whispered, his hands lightly framing her shoulders. "I want you to know, I love you for it."

Chapter Four

They were standing very close—little more than a breath apart—and the attraction between them was too powerful to resist. Circumstances and Seth's sleek but nondescript kitchen with its pizza remains and after-dinner clutter receded, until the two of them were marooned on an island in time and space. Like one bemused or bewitched, Margo felt Seth's arms come around her. The palms of her hands settled against the soft, nubby texture of his sweater as he lowered his mouth to hers.

From the moment they'd met, amid the damp and paint fumes and bustle of Danner Yachts, Inc., she'd had the uncanny feeling that he was someone she *knew*—a missing piece of her life's puzzle. Thanks to Sooz and Beth, she was convinced their destinies were intertwined like lovers. With a little sigh of surrender, she shut her eyes.

At first he nuzzled her with tentative ardor, his mouth barely brushing hers, though it was hot and sweet.

Hushed and bursting with promise, the moment couldn't last. Margo caught her breath as Seth drew back, hesitated, and then kissed her again with more blatant hunger, questing and tasting as if she were some hitherto untried delicacy that he planned to savor to the utmost.

Overcome by the splendor of what he was making her feel, she wanted to melt into him, lose herself in the wonder that he was. Caution and common sense abandoned her, and she parted her lips.

My God! Seth thought, going hard in an instant. She's incredible. Generous and nurturing, yet as volatile as a Gypsy. Her warm, wet mouth was like ambrosia to him as he probed its depths with his tongue.

In that passionate embrace, the extent of Seth's arousal wasn't any secret. Though Margo could keep her body's response hidden better than he could, she was helpless before the avalanche of need that surged in her blood. She longed to wrap herself around him.

Afterward, she couldn't have said how long they stood there by the sink, blurring and blending into the knowledge of how much they wanted each other. She only knew it was paradise to her. By contrast, she hadn't been fully alive for years.

It was like a dousing of cold water, then, or a sudden jolt of electricity when Sooz's little-girl voice rang out.

"Daddy? Can you come up and help me with my arithmetic?"

As if they'd been caught in some illicit, unpardonable act, they hastily jumped apart. Margo's heart was beating like a sledgehammer, but they hadn't been discovered. Sooz had shouted her request from the top of the stairs the way she usually did, rather than appearing in the kitchen to ask her father face-to-face.

The fire in Seth's tawny, king-of-the-jungle eyes was banked but far from extinguished. Margo had wanted him as much as he'd wanted her and it was too late for her to pretend otherwise. He didn't plan to let her off the hook, either. "Back in a minute," he said, giving her upper arms a possessive little squeeze before he left the room.

Shaken, Margo rinsed and stacked the dishes and her baking utensils as she tried to get hold of herself. Never, not even in her late husband's arms, had she felt so bonded to a man, so erotically stimulated. By now she knew what she'd only guessed at before. Making love to Seth Danner would be like burning to a white-hot ingot. A woman would emerge from the cauldron of his embrace even more herself, yet forever changed. Everything in her was aching to experience it. She couldn't remember wanting anything so much.

Yet how could she justify indulging herself? Love couldn't be built on a lie and she was an imposter in Seth's house—a stranger passing herself off as a single father's dream of a housekeeper, when in reality she was on a fact-finding mission that could forever change their lives. If and when Seth discovered her motive for agreeing to cook and clean for him, or once she was forced to tell him, they wouldn't stand a chance.

There weren't enough dishes to bother turning on the dishwasher and, with a sigh, Margo ran a sinkful of suds. In her opinion, Seth was the kind of impassioned, demonstrative yet sustaining and trustworthy man every woman dreamed about meeting and loving someday. Though she hadn't been looking for anyone in a romantic sense, she'd found him. And maybe, just maybe, he was genuinely attracted to her. Why not keep quiet and see what happens? she thought. Seth's unattached, and you have a perfect right to know if Sooz is your natural daughter. You wouldn't be harming anyone if you let matters take their natural course.

As Margo scrubbed the cookie sheets, her conscience argued that getting involved with Seth would be disloyal to Sooz. She's the reason you're here, Margo reminded herself. All your focus should be on her. Later, if the truth comes out and you've kept your relationship with him on a business footing, at least he won't feel betrayed in a man-woman sense.

She'd have to reach an understanding with him—and fast—before they ended up in each other's arms again. "Back in a minute" had definite connotations of taking up where they left off. And she was hardly immune.

Margo was waiting for Seth in the living room when he came back downstairs. Perched nervously on the hassock that matched his black leather and teak Eames Chair, she got to her feet.

He could see at once that she'd thrown up barriers.

"Margo, I . . ." he began.

She wouldn't let him finish. "What happened in the kitchen a little while ago was nobody's fault," she said, keeping her voice low so Sooz wouldn't overhear. "But it was a major mistake. It's part of my job to care for your daughter and I've just begun to establish a relationship with her. It's still fragile and I don't want anything to spoil it. If she caught us . . . *embracing* like that . . . she'd conclude I was trying to take over her father, that I had no real interest in her."

Standing there looking up at him from the downhill end of the eleven-inch disparity in their heights, with determination glowing in her dark eyes and her lipstick all but obliterated by the ministrations of his mouth, Margo was a tempting sight. Seth wanted her, damn it! Distractedly helping Sooz with her math, he'd been eager as a high school kid sunk in his first romance to taste Margo again and see if the delicious surrender she'd offered was fact or a figment of his imagination. The urge to sweep aside her objections and let passion have its way warred with reluctant understanding on his face.

Sooz will have to accept another woman in my life eventually. It might as well be now, he thought. Yet he had to admit Margo had a point. If he knew his daughter, Margo's assessment of her probable reaction to anything approaching an affair of the heart between them was right on target.

Because of the employer-employee relationship in which they found themselves, there was also the question of propriety. He didn't want to put Margo in an awkward position.

"You're right," he agreed, setting aside his own needs and desires. "I was completely out of line, coming on to you the way I did. Sooz and I need you here, and I don't want to do anything to drive you away. I promise I'll do my best not to let it happen again."

It wasn't an ironclad guarantee. Still, for the next few weeks, Seth made himself scarce, staying late at the boat yard almost every night and carting off his warmed-over supper to his office when he returned to the house on Magnolia Boulevard. In the mornings, he snatched his breakfast on the run.

Now and then, he paused to exchange a few words with her about Sooz. Whenever he did, the regret she felt over the wall that had sprung up between them intensified. He was sexy, caring, a man who radiated a special resonance all his own. Each time their hands accidentally touched, or they brushed against each other in passing, her attraction to him deepened. Apparently he planned to keep his word and his distance, but in her secret heart, where common sense played only a minor role, she didn't want him to.

At least she was making progress with Sooz. The girl had thawed to the point where she hung about after school most days, helping Margo fix dinner and begging for more paper dolls, unless she was doing homework or playing outdoors. Day by day, Margo's affection for the energetic, outspoken moppet grew. Though she continued to miss Beth Ann and regard the elfin, dark-haired child she'd lost as her own little girl, she had to admit Sooz was helping heal the hurt.

We're a long way from having a mother-daughter relationship, Margo commented to herself one rainy afternoon as she taught Sooz how to sew in the process of helping her mend her precious "Bear's" ripped taffeta vest. Yet, little by little, we're becoming friends. Though Sooz will never take Beth's place in my heart, she seems to be creating one of her own.

It was the Friday before Thanksgiving. Several hours later, as Margo was about to slip out the door and head home for a weekend of playing catch-up with her sadly neglected desktop publishing business, Seth laid a detaining hand on her arm. He was wearing a maize fisherman-style sweater that emphasized the natural highlights in his reddish-gold hair. The well-worn trousers in a nut-brown corduroy he'd chosen to go with it fit snugly. They did nothing to hide his narrow hips and powerful leg muscles.

Just to have him touch her again after yearning for heaven out of reach made her knees go weak. She could feel the sensual pull of him like a magnet.

"Yes?" she managed.

"I wonder if I could talk to you for a moment?"

Sooz was upstairs, getting ready for an evening out with him. She wouldn't overhear. Meanwhile Margo was keenly aware that, once again, Seth had invaded her personal space. He was so big, so warm and muscular, and he smelled so good. The tang of his after-shave and skin-scent teased her nostrils.

"What about?" she asked, concentrating on his disarming fringe of blond lashes to keep from getting lost in his eyes.

It's a lot to ask, Seth thought. I don't know anything about her life away from here. But, what the heck? I might as well give it a try.

He gestured with one big, beautifully proportioned hand. "About the coming holiday..."

"Yes?"

"Naturally, it's yours if you want it. But if you don't have any special plans, maybe you'd consider taking a different day off at your convenience and hanging around to fix a turkey for us. Sooz hasn't been part of anything like that for ages. I know it would mean a great deal to her."

Though it was equally accurate, he didn't add that it would mean a great deal to him, as well. To the best of his recollection, Cheryl had never fixed a traditional holiday meal, preferring that they dine at the home of relatives or in a first-class restaurant. He was charmed by the notion of turkey roasting in his own kitchen and Margo smiling at him over the assembled feast.

As she approached her first major holiday without Beth, who'd died the previous January, Margo hadn't been looking forward to much of a celebration. Hoping to stem the tide of painful memories she expected to assail her, she'd decided to prepare a capon at her Ravenna bungalow and invite Nell over, since her friend's beau would be out of town. But now that an opportunity had arisen to spend the day with Seth and Sooz, a little flame of anticipation curled to life inside her.

"To tell you the truth, it sounds like fun," she admitted. "If I hadn't planned to invite a friend over—"

Seth's light-colored brows drew together in a frown. I might have guessed she'd be cooking for a man, he thought, pushing down the prickling of jealousy he felt. "Say no more," he cut in. "You've been very generous with your free time already and we don't want to impose."

"It's just that her gentleman friend plans to spend the day with his family in Portland," Margo explained. "And she doesn't have any close relatives west of the Alleghenies."

Her *gentleman* friend? Wonder of wonders, Margo's prospective dinner guest was female. "By all means, ask her to join us, if that's the only thing stopping you," he said, flashing her a smile that was like the sun reappearing from behind a cloud. "I'd like to invite my brother and sister-in-law, as well. They've entertained us so many times I've lost count and it's time to repay the favor. Besides, I enjoy a houseful of people underfoot on holidays."

Eager to have Nell meet the Danners, Margo phoned her right away. As she'd expected, her friend snapped up the invitation. All weekend long, as Margo sat at her computer and struggled to pay attention to the brochures and newsletters she'd promised to get out as soon as possible, her mind wanted to focus on pumpkin pies and cranberry sauce. She kept daydreaming about stuffing the festive bird with Sooz's help, and watching Seth beam at everyone in that benign, masterful way he had from the head of his dining-room table.

When Sooz got home from school on Tuesday, Margo asked her if she'd like to go along to the market and help pick out the turkey. "It's quite a responsibility, you know," she added, "getting just the right one."

Sooz's eyes widened. "Could I really?"

Margo risked a hug. "I wouldn't ask if I didn't want your help. But I warn you . . . we have lots of other groceries to get. And my car's pretty small. On the way home, some of them might end up in your lap."

Seth wasn't due home for quite a while, and for once Sooz didn't have homework. If they got going immediately, they'd be back by dinnertime. Bundled up against the damp, chilly weather, they emerged from the house to find Seth's Mercedes pulling into the drive.

"Daddy! What are you doing home?" Sooz exclaimed as he turned off the engine and got out.

Playfully, Seth pulled her knit cap down around her ears. "I live here, remember? The question is, where are you two ladies going with such eager expressions on your faces?"

By now Sooz was literally bouncing up and down with excitement. "We're going to get the turkey! Please . . . *pretty please*. Come with us!"

Still smiling, Seth quirked a questioning brow at Margo.

"It might take quite a while," she said. "We've got a lot of stuff to get."

"In that case, you need a bigger car to haul it in. And an extra pair of hands. Allow me to volunteer my services."

Nothing about her experience to date had prompted Margo to view Seth as the domestic type. Yet he truly

seemed to enjoy sizing up the plumpest, most promising
birds at her favorite market, not to mention checking out
the cauliflower, fresh cranberries, spices, homemade
mincemeat and extensive wine selection.

Sooz was in seventh heaven. It was impossible not to
smile as she dashed between her father and Margo, tout-
ing this or that discovery and adding more selections to
their already overflowing cart.

I know it's dangerous to think this way, Margo admitted to herself, but we're almost like a family. I can feel
happiness settling into place around me. Well aware that
relationships built on deception had two strikes against
them from the outset, she was nonetheless tempted to
hope, as Seth bought her and Sooz each a bouquet of
freesias on their way out of the market, that the mixup
that had drawn them together might quietly resolve itself.

Thanksgiving dawned misty and overcast, a muted
watercolor of a day still glistening with wash. Not a trace
of unfiltered light—the equivalent of bright, white paper—showed through. Puget Sound was like blue milk,
its islands mysterious blue-green shapes. In the shipping
lanes, a barge was running with its lights on. The far-off
mountains of the Olympic Peninsula were obliterated by
clouds.

In an effort to counteract the gloom, Seth built a fire
and put some classical music on the stereo. To Margo's
surprise, a few minutes later he joined her and Sooz in the
kitchen. A domesticated lion that morning, he offered to
clean celery and onions and run the food-processor while
she and Sooz rinsed the turkey and got out an assortment of spices and bread crumbs for the dressing.

Margo didn't expect him to. Yet, once the bird was stuffed, trussed, patted lovingly by Sooz and nestled in its roasting pan, Seth stayed around, cleaning up after them as they made pumpkin and mincemeat pies. At Margo's suggestion, Sooz used the pastry scraps to fashion little jam-filled tarts, which she proudly rolled out herself. Blissfully flour-dusted, with assorted cooking stains on her apron and a streak of jam on her chin, the dark-haired child who'd initially been so unwelcoming to Margo was a model of friendliness and cooperation.

"Thanks," Seth mouthed behind Sooz's back as, with Margo hovering over her for safety's sake, Sooz pulled the cookie sheet with her finished tarts on it from one of the twin ovens.

"My pleasure," Margo's smile replied. She'd had some bad moments on awakening, over Beth's loss. Yet most of her emotions that morning were happy ones. Despite her fears over where it could lead, her feeling of connectedness to Seth and Sooz continued to grow. A strong affection for both of them was putting down permanent roots in her heart.

At last they adjourned to the living room to drink hot chocolate, watch Macy's parade on television and play Chinese checkers in front of the fire. Gradually the turkey began to permeate the air with its heavenly aroma. By the time it was at the point where it needed basting, Seth had settled back with a bowl of popcorn to watch football. Between trips to the kitchen, Margo and Sooz flopped cozily on the couch nearby to leaf through the Christmas catalogs.

Around 4:00 p.m., Nell arrived and was properly introduced. After a few minutes' conversation with Seth, Margo's friend gave her an approving look. The sparkle in Nell's eyes didn't diminish when her gaze rested on

Sooz. It was easy to see that Nell agreed: Sooz was a treasure in her own right and very likely Margo's missing daughter.

An hour or so later, they set the table. Since Seth's brother and partner, Bob Danner, and his wife, Joy, were childless, Margo barely gave it a second thought when she assigned them two places. No one had mentioned they might bring a guest.

In her room, changing from slacks and a sweater to her favorite emerald-green velvet holiday dress, Margo heard *two* unfamiliar female voices in the entryway as Seth welcomed them. She descended the stairs to find Joy's divorced cousin, Samantha, hanging flirtatiously on Seth's arm.

Though Samantha lived and worked in Bellingham, apparently she and Seth had met several times before. Throughout the meal, which earned raves from everyone, the pretty if somewhat jaded looking blonde seemed bent on ingratiating herself with Seth and Sooz—apparently with Bob's and Joy's blessing. Sooz responded warily, obviously scenting strong competition for her father's attention. Relaxed and affable, Seth gave every indication of basking in Samantha's regard.

Irked though she didn't have any claim on him, Margo remembered Nell's comment about Leo men. "If you want to win one over," she'd said, "be his audience." Though she hadn't been privy to that advice, Samantha seemed to be following it.

According to Nell's analysis, Seth needed a mate to be happy in life, and it seemed Samantha agreed. Unfortunately, after making it clear to him that their relationship mustn't go beyond the casual friendliness of employer and employee, Margo was in no position to protest.

* * *

Saturday was Sooz's ninth birthday, just as it would have been Beth's. Expecting to spend the day at home, alone and depressed, Margo let Seth talk her into a boat trip that—thanks to warmer weather—would culminate in a cookout-birthday party at a cottage he and his brother owned near the village of Friday Harbor on San Juan Island.

"We've already laid claim to most of your holiday...you might as well devote the rest of it to us," he said with a grin when Sooz got into the act and begged her to come along.

Provided they got an early start, it would be an easy day trip north of Seattle on Seth's thirty-foot power yacht, which he kept at the boatworks. Several of Sooz's school friends and their parents had been invited, as well as her Uncle Bob and Aunt Joy. Having learned Samantha would be spending the weekend with them, Margo wasn't too surprised when the pair arrived with her in tow.

Deciding it would be emotional suicide to compete, Margo turned her attention to getting Sooz and her friends settled in the stern as everyone boarded the yacht. To her chagrin, she was only partly successful in ignoring Samantha's blatant campaign. As they left Lake Union and the Lake Washington ship canal behind to pass through the massive Hiram M. Chittenden locks, she was treated to the sight of the seductively attired blonde fraternizing with Seth on the bridge while she and Bob tossed temporary mooring lines to the blue-uniformed attendants.

The trip up, via Puget Sound and the San Juan archipelago, was almost beautiful enough to distract her. San Juan and its sister islands, including Shaw and Orcas, were situated in the so-called rain shadow of Mt. Olympus and they were traditionally sunnier than Seattle. Before long the sun appeared, glinting off the snowcap on distant Mt. Rainier and sparkling on ice-cold water that foamed aquamarine in their wake. The islands themselves, humping like partially submerged whales, were the color of emeralds.

The Danner cottage, on San Juan's southeastern shore, had been built of redwood and sat atop a steep, forested bluff. Because of the disparity between high and low tide in that area, Seth had told Margo, it had a floating dock and ramp. These led to a narrow wooden staircase that zigzagged up the bluff face.

A stranger to everyone but Seth and Sooz, Margo did her best to serve as hostess, passing out snacks and soft drinks and making polite conversation as he cleaned up the outdoor grill for a barbecue. But she didn't *feel* self-effacing. Inside she was steaming. Seth Danner's too good for you, she told his sister-in-law's cousin silently as the woman teased and flirted with him.

As the afternoon wore on, it appeared that, for Margo, the only high point of the day would be Sooz's delight when she opened her gifts. Cuddling the rag doll that Margo had fashioned in her image, complete with miniature flannel pajamas that resembled the kind she usually wore, Sooz flung her arms around Margo and gave her a resounding kiss on the cheek.

"This doll comes with a special offer, you know," Margo said with a lump in her throat.

Open by now to considering almost any deal Margo cared to suggest, Sooz demanded an explanation.

"If you take extra good care of her," Margo explained, "on Christmas morning, you'll find more clothes for her under the tree."

Sooz's dark eyes danced with anticipation. "I will, Margo. I promise!" she exclaimed.

Flattered by Samantha's attention, though she wasn't his type, Seth watched his daughter and Margo interact with pleasure. In his opinion, Sooz hadn't looked as happy and secure since she was a toddler. Margo's been good for both of us, he thought, though it's impossible to live under the same roof with her and not want to kiss her until she melts. I wonder what it would take to change her mind about us....

Maybe he was imagining things, but he had the distinct impression that she wasn't too happy over Samantha's flirtation with him. And then there'd been that incident in the kitchen. She'd participated fully, no mistake. So she had to be interested.

It was an unseasonably warm afternoon, considering the month and the latitude. With Sooz's birthday cake reduced to crumbs and the children off to play a game of tag among the trees, the adults pitched in to dispose of the debris, then settled back in a motley collection of outdoor chairs for coffee and conversation. Clinging to Seth like a leech, Samantha claimed the place of honor beside him on an Adirondack-style wooden bench.

That tears it, thought Margo in disgust. I can't take any more of this. My voluntary duties as hostess are about finished and I need a few minutes to myself. Mentioning something about going down to the yacht to retrieve a sweater, she descended the wooden staircase that led to the water.

About halfway down, hidden by the bluff from the party above, she paused and leaned over the railing. Waves were washing to shore from the wake of the Anacortes–San Juan ferry as it made for Friday Harbor and she didn't hear Seth's footsteps on the weathered planking behind her. She jumped when he put his arms around her waist.

"You startled me!" she exclaimed, turning to face him. "Did I?"

His murmur was husky and intimate, and—if she really wanted to keep him at arm's length—the maneuver had been a mistake. Desperately, she racked her brain for something to say.

"I was just on my way down to get a sweater..."

Seth lowered his head. She could feel his breath on her like a caress.

"So I understood," he said. "I came after you to say that you won't need it...not with me to keep you warm."

Any protest she might have voiced was forgotten as his mouth took possession of hers. In an instant the afternoon's frustrations were swept aside. Screened from the eyes of Sooz's birthday guests and lost in a green-and-blue world of fir trees and water, they touched and tasted. With each thrust of his tongue and heated response from hers, they moved deeper into a wilderness of passion from which ultimately there might be no retreat.

At last Seth drew back and looked at her.

"I thought...we weren't going to do that again," she whispered.

"So did I," he admitted, placing a light kiss on the tip of her nose. "But then I seem to be fairly weak-willed where you're concerned. Tell you what... I'm ready to break the rules whenever you are. I'll leave the time and place of our next infraction up to you."

Chapter Five

During the next few days, Sooz seemed to open like the petals of a flower under Margo's influence. Humbled by the girl's trust and aware she didn't fully deserve it, Margo realized she'd gone from curiosity and exasperation to loving her very much. Though she didn't dare ask for the genetic tissue test that would prove it, she was almost one hundred percent certain Sooz was hers, the child she'd carried in her womb.

Her feelings for the girl raised a question she couldn't avoid indefinitely—namely, whether to give Sooz up, tell Seth the truth and risk alienating him, or settle for something in between. She couldn't continue as the family housekeeper forever, even if she were willing to consign her desktop publishing business to the scrap heap. Ultimately, living on the fringe of Sooz's life wouldn't be enough.

There was also the problem of Seth. With each passing day, her desire and affection for the tall, redheaded yacht builder grew. His kiss on the wooden steps leading down to the water from his vacation cottage and the challenge of sorts that had followed it had done everything to excite and unsettle her and done nothing for her peace of mind.

If she'd understood him correctly, he didn't intend the interplay of sensual possibilities between them to end there. Though she'd escaped back up the bluff, deciding she didn't need a sweater after all, his tawny eyes had followed her. "When are you going to give up and admit we're fatally attracted to each other?" they'd seemed to ask as she'd moved self-consciously among his guests. "A divorced father shouldn't have to walk on eggs forever. Why can't you care about us both?"

The unresolved tension between them had only increased since they'd returned to Seattle. Every look, every unspoken comment from Seth prompted her to commit the next "infraction," as he'd put it. Soon, something would have to give.

As the weekend approached, Margo thought she might get a breather. Seth's ex-wife, Cheryl, and her new husband, Tom Magnuson, were scheduled to breeze into town on Saturday for a couple of days before flying on to Chicago. The inevitable awkwardness of their visit should take Seth's focus off *her* for a while.

During their stay, Seth had agreed to let Sooz sleep over with her mother and stepfather at a downtown hotel. Supposedly a belated birthday celebration was in the works. Though she hadn't worked for the Danners long, Margo had already guessed how the Cheryl-Sooz equation worked. Stingy with her time and attention, Cheryl gave lots of expensive presents.

As Saturday drew near, Sooz's excitement escalated until she was all but jumping out of her skin. There's no need to be jealous, Margo reminded herself with only partial success as she prepared to depart for her Ravenna bungalow. You can't expect to assume Cheryl's place in Sooz's heart any more than she could have supplanted you with Beth.

She couldn't help being a little envious, though, of the woman Sooz clearly loved so much. How could Cheryl have given up her daughter so easily, and settled for infrequent visits? According to Harry Spence, custody had never been an issue.

In fact, how could Cheryl have given up Seth?

Sooz rushed to answer the door Saturday morning when Cheryl and Tom arrived—fully two hours late. From his office, where he'd holed up to avoid the initial drama of the mother-daughter reunion, Seth could hear his daughter's fervent squeals of delight. They were accompanied by Cheryl's effervescent laughter and Tom Magnuson's affable, slightly nervous boom.

Seth had nothing against Tom, though the wealthy real estate magnate had been seeing his ex-wife while she was still married to him. The person he blamed for that blatant lapse of decency was Cheryl. As his wife, she had owed him loyalty and a certain amount of respect. The least she could have done was let him know before going out and finding herself another, wealthier husband.

It's my damn pride, Seth acknowledged ruefully, putting aside the estimate he'd been working on. He'd lived long enough to realize that the need to avoid embarrassment and ridicule was one of his biggest stumbling blocks. Maybe seeing Cheryl again would be easier if he remembered she'd done him a favor by leaving him.

His ex-wife and her new husband were ultra-polite when he entered the living room. About to offer his hand,

Tom Magnuson apparently thought better of it and thrust it back into his pocket. Sooz, of course, was jumping up and down, hanging onto her mother. Though she had eyes only for Cheryl, Seth knew his daughter's keen ability in picking up unfriendly vibes between her parents only too well. She'd detect—and be upset by—the slightest hint of discord.

"Hi, Cheryl...Tom. How are you?" Seth greeted them, doing his best to be magnanimous. "You're both looking well."

After they'd gone, taking Sooz with them, he was at loose ends. Though Margo had enlivened its decor, adding a few colorful pillows here, and an afghan there, without her and his daughter, the house seemed empty. He considered finishing the estimate he'd started. Or putting in some extra time at the boat yard. Neither idea appealed to him. Throughout the week, the weather had continued unseasonably warm and clear. It was a fine day for an outing. Except for Sooz, there was only one person he wanted to spend it with.

Busy playing catch-up on her computer, Margo frowned when the doorbell rang. Darn, she thought, somebody trying to sell me something. Then she softened her irritation. Maybe her caller was a Brownie or a Girl Scout, hoping to land a cookie order.

Her eyes widened as she opened the door. "Seth!" she exclaimed, staring up at him in astonishment. "What are you doing here? Is anything wrong?"

He shrugged, not quite sure of his welcome. "Not really. The house seemed kind of empty with Sooz gone. I got lonesome."

For whatever reason, he'd turned to her. A warm little flame of pleasure curled to life inside her. At the same time, she shuddered as she took mental inventory of herself and the home that had become something of a weekend getaway.

Seth had chosen to arrive, unannounced, at her usually tidy bungalow on a morning when she'd barely combed her hair and had left the previous night's dishes soaking in the sink. Some housekeeper she'd turned out to be on her own turf! And some glamour girl—she hadn't even put on lipstick!

"Aren't you going to ask me in?" he said.

Head-over-heels crazy about him, Margo couldn't send him away, though she was well aware that being alone with him meant flirting with danger.

"Of course," she answered, stepping aside so he could enter. "It's just that you startled me, turning up out of the blue like this. Promise me you'll keep your eyes closed. Or at the very least, excuse the way I look. I'm afraid the house is a bit of a mess, too. I let things slide so I could finish up some work..."

If she expected him to keep his eyes shut, then she'd have to lead him around by the hand. Come to think of it, if she did that, he'd be justified groping in support. But while it was an entrancing idea, he wasn't willing to forego the satisfaction of looking her over from head to toe. She was positively scrumptious this morning in a baggy sweatshirt with no apparent bra beneath it, and form-fitting, faded jeans that were fraying at the knees. He ached to sweep her off her feet.

"I know I should have called first," he admitted with the beginnings of a grin as he glanced around her cozy living room with its white brick fireplace, multiple shelves of books and overstuffed couch upholstered in a rose-and-white tulip pattern, then back at her. "Of course, you might have said no. Have you had breakfast? All I managed this morning was a cup of instant coffee and a stale doughnut.''

Margo realized he wasn't complaining. He was just being a typical man: semi-helpless in the kitchen and more than willing to let someone take care of him, preferably a woman. Distracted by his strong male allure, she tried to picture the contents of her refrigerator. Now that she was gone five days out of seven, its contents were pretty meager. She'd just been thinking she ought to do some shopping.

"I'm afraid I don't have much in the way of groceries on hand," she admitted. "If we're lucky, I might be able to rustle you up some scrambled eggs and toast."

It was nearly noon. And Seth hadn't driven across town simply so she could cook for him. He resisted the urge to pull her into his arms and place a warm little kiss on the tip of her nose.

"I thought we might go out," he answered. "For lunch. My treat. The weather's great and, afterward, we could bum around awhile. That is, if you have time and I wouldn't be taking you away from anything important."

Margo had turned out no work the previous weekend. If she took Seth up on his invitation, she'd have to beg for an extension on the Peterson project. And, though she'd probably get it, there were other pitfalls. The kind of "going out" he had in mind would permanently transform the nature of their relationship.

Well, what was life anyway but a series of risks? If getting closer to Seth was a mistake, she'd pay the price. At the moment, it felt exactly right.

"There's nothing I can't finish later," she decided, running her fingers through her tousled mane of curls in a preliminary effort to tame them. "If you don't mind waiting, I'll run and change."

Seth had dressed casually in loafers, tan corduroy slacks, a cream-colored cable-knit sweater and a bomber-style leather jacket. Pouring on the steam, Margo raced and shucked her disreputable working clothes and pawed frantically through her closet. She wanted to look her best!

Shifting his attention from a collection of family photographs arranged on a table as she came running back, Seth couldn't believe the speed or extent of her transformation. For her day of "bumming" around with him, Margo had chosen a schoolgirl tartan that ended at mid-thigh. Its pleats swished flirtatiously above shapely legs clad in demure red tights. A tailored white blouse left open at the throat and a red wool-velour blazer completed her outfit. The flat skimmers she wore only added to her youthful look.

She could be Sooz's older sister, Seth thought. They even look alike. But he knew Margo's age; she'd mentioned it when she'd applied for work with him. She was thirty-one—just seven years shy of his own randy and still youthful thirty-eight. No problem there.

"You look terrific," he said, meaning it.

So do you, she wanted to answer. Something about the way he stood gazing down at her, with his six foot, two inch frame taking up an inordinate amount of space in her tiny living room, made her heart turn over. It was like having a magnificent and only partly domesticated wild animal under her roof. Maybe even eating out of her hand. Seth Danner, king of the jungle, she thought fondly, remembering his August birthday and the chart Nell had drawn up for him. You're the quintessential Leo man.

* * *

At Seth's suggestion, they drove to Pike Place, Seattle's revamped covered market situated between the downtown skyscrapers and the port. By sheer luck, he managed to find a parking place for the Mercedes on a nearby street.

"I thought we might try the Athenian Café," he murmured, taking firm possession of Margo's hand and leading her inside, past crowded produce stalls where every apple was polished and every bunch of broccoli beaded with water droplets.

As usual, the stall keepers could easily have been mistaken for carnival barkers as they touted the quality and low cost of their wares. The hawkers of fresh seafood, including Dungeness crab and pink-hued salmon on beds of crushed ice, seemed even more intent on showmanship.

Joining the throng of shoppers and tourists who wandered the market's narrow aisles, Margo and Seth skirted T-shirt vendors and displays of exotic spices, a Chinese fast-food counter and racks of foreign magazines. A youngish, bearded man with a guitar was singing religious songs and accepting contributions. A woman passed out leaflets advertising a free peace concert. From his vantage point atop his father's shoulders, a toddler in a bunny suit stared at the shifting scene with solemn eyes.

The Athenian—bustling, smoky and somewhat dark except for a double tier of window booths overlooking the water—offered an oasis of sorts. It had an old-fashioned square lunch counter with round, chrome and red leatherette stools. Honey-soaked Greek pastries glistened on paper-lace doilies in domed and footed glass dishes. A huge copper samovar, no longer used to dispense coffee, was part of the restaurant's ambiance.

Seth tipped the hostess to ensure them a window seat. "This has to be one of the best views of Elliott Bay from downtown...at least from street level," he remarked, sliding onto the bench opposite hers though he'd have preferred to sit beside her.

Scarcely able to believe they were actually spending the day together, Margo smiled back at him. "You're right," she agreed, noting with pleasure the little laugh lines at the corners of his eyes and the generous proportions of his mouth. "Today you can see the mountains. With the sun on their peaks, they're just a shade darker than the sky."

Though the menu featured a variety of main dishes and accompaniments ranging from seafood fettucine to Jugoslav potatoes, they settled for Greek salads, conversation and a glass of retsina each. When they'd finished, Seth suggested they descend through the market's lower levels to the port and play tourist by visiting the city's famed aquarium.

They were employee and employer. Amateur sleuth and an unwitting target of her clandestine quest for information. The questions of Sooz's parentage and Margo's failure to tell the truth about her motives stood ready to separate them. But Margo didn't want to think about that. For a day, an hour, the next few minutes, if that's all she was destined to have with him, she wanted to live in the present.

"Sounds great," she answered, pushing guilt back into its subterranean hiding place.

Hand in hand, they scrambled down seemingly endless steps to emerge in sunlight. Across the trolley tracks and busy Alaskan Way was the city's popular waterfront promenade with its fish 'n' chip eateries, souvenir shops, harbor tour ticket booths and ferry docks.

"Did you change your mind?" Margo asked when Seth tugged her to a halt on the wooden decking outside the aquarium entrance.

His hands spanned her waist. "I know I promised to let you choose the time and place for our next infraction, but I can't wait."

They were in full public view—center stage with the city for a backdrop—as he took possession of her mouth. By now his warmth, the incomparable taste of him, had become as necessary to her as light and breath. Straining on tiptoe, she returned his kiss full measure. Time slowed, pouring out like honey as their tongues made contact.

How much deeper in each other could they get? They both knew the answer: a *lot* deeper. At last Seth drew back and looked at her. A forest fire of need was raging in his tawny eyes.

"You know, don't you," he growled, "that you're habit forming?"

Still drowning in the exquisite morass of feelings he'd evoked, Margo wasn't sure how to answer him. She only knew she wanted them to go on touching.

Seth had similar aspirations. Though she'd failed to confirm what they'd just shared in words, her capitulation and the way she continued to let him hold her told him everything he thought he needed to know. "Let's go inside," he said gruffly, staking his claim with one possessive arm about her shoulders.

That afternoon, the aquarium's dim, underwater light, the echoing voices of children and tank after tank of exotic sea life took on a surreal quality Margo would never forget. It was almost as if the sharks, clown fish and sea anemones they viewed had originated on another planet.

All her real attention was focused on Seth. With a yearning that sprang from some primitive place inside her, she longed to kiss him again and again until they were both drunk with it. Yet it was magical, too, just being with him. Where before she'd existed separately in the world, for today, at least, the two of them were a couple.

As they stood in semi-darkness, watching sunlight filter through an overhead tank of frantically swimming salmon "fingerlings," Margo dared to slip an arm about his waist. In response, he drew her closer. Lovers come here, she thought. Later, they return as husband and wife to explain the sea's wonders to their children. If her suspicions were correct, she and Seth already shared a child, though they hadn't created her together in love.

From the aquarium, they took a streetcar to the International District, where they browsed through Uwajimaya, a huge Oriental grocery-hardware store, then crossed the street so Seth could purchase a mango sponge cake, the specialty of a bakery he knew.

"You don't seriously expect us to eat the whole thing?" Margo protested in mock dismay as they walked back to the trolley terminus.

"We could have a food fight with it when we get back to your house," he answered imperturbably, holding the cake box upright in one hand while making sure she stayed close beside him with the other. "But these cakes are pretty fabulous. If you've never tasted one, maybe you'd better sample it first."

The day was cool enough for his purchase to keep without refrigeration. When they reached the Mercedes again, Seth proposed drinks atop the Space Needle at Seattle Center. "We can make it coffee if you like," he said. "After spending most of the day at sea level, I have an overwhelming urge to lay the city at your feet."

In the Needle's revolving restaurant, they shared cappuccinos and held hands as the sun dipped in the west to disappear in a streak of pure beaten gold. Studded with more and more lights, the city's cozy, identifiable hills assumed their nocturnal glitter as the dusk deepened to indigo. Downtown, the cluster of tall buildings that thrust skyward, was paved with diamonds.

Consulting each other's taste, they discovered they both liked jazz. They wound up having a casual supper at Dimitriou's Jazz Alley and hanging around for part of the show. At last they were back at Margo's door.

It was the classic moment of truth. Should she ask him in? Though the same troublesome caveats that had bothered her earlier still applied, there wasn't any real doubt in her mind. She couldn't let him go without another taste of what had pleased them both so much.

"My fireplace isn't as elegant as yours, but I have a few birch logs and some cognac left over from an impulse buy last winter," she said. "Would you care to partake?"

She didn't have to extend the invitation twice.

Unlocking her front door, Seth tossed his jacket over a chair and set about building a fire while she took off her shoes, stowed the mango cake in the refrigerator and poured out their drinks.

Their fingers brushed as she handed him a miniature snifter, half filled with potent amber liquid, and her inner glow of excitement deepened. "Any musical preference?" she asked casually, placing her snifter on the coffee table and going over to the stereo.

Seth had kicked off his loafers. He was padding about in his woolly socks. "You choose," he replied, taking a seat on the couch next to the one she'd staked out. "Mind if I appropriate one of these throw pillows and put up my feet?''

A warm little shiver of anticipation coursed through her. "Be my guest."

Selecting Ray Lynch's compact disc, "Deep Breakfast," which she set to repeat at low volume, Margo returned to his side. It seemed the most natural thing in the world that he should slip an arm around her.

There was nobody else about, no beloved but difficult Sooz to catch them and take offense. The lamp they'd turned on when they arrived had a three-way bulb and Seth had switched it to low. Its diffuse illumination didn't compete with the romance of the firelight as they sipped at their cognacs and set them aside.

Seconds later, they were in each other's arms.

"God, how I want you," Seth confessed, pulling her onto his lap and crushing her mouth with his. "Being so close to you all day... it's made me crazy."

Margo wanted him too—a thousand times more desperately than she'd known it was possible to want someone. "I know," she admitted when he gave her a chance to speak. "I felt the same way."

It was as if an avalanche had been set in motion. Fierce and tender, with the finesse of heaven's most accomplished archangel, Seth probed her mouth's moist privacy with his tongue in imitation of the act of love. Every ounce of fervor Margo possessed welcomed him. Encouraged not to stop at barriers, he inserted one hand beneath her blouse, then inside the lacy scrap of her bra. She moaned softly as he stroked her nipples to taut readiness.

Flooded though she was with mind-blowing sensations, she knew what they were ready for: the sweet marauding tug of his mouth. She wanted to give him

everything—every womanly attribute and soul-satisfying
pleasure that could take shape in her imagination. Poised
on the brink of complete abandonment, she gloried in the
hard sensation of his thighs beneath her buttocks.

You mustn't do this, the voice of reason pleaded,
struggling to be heard. You have to think of Sooz, and
where your deception of Seth might lead. Do you want
to love him only to lose him? The woman who lusted so
hotly in her refused to be satisfied with crumbs. Or logic.
It's been nine years, that sensual, reckless woman argued. You deserve a night of happiness. In the morning,
you can work things out.

To her surprise, it was Seth who called a halt. Taking
a deep breath, he removed his hand from beneath her
blouse and cuddled her head against his shoulder.

"Don't I...please you?" she faltered, her cheeks going scarlet.

"Ah, Margo..." With a little shake of his head, Seth
tightened his hold. "I want more from you than an hour
of bliss, followed by your resignation in the morning.
That's why I won't make love to you so precipitously.
But, if you'll let me, I'd like to spend the night."

Chapter Six

Reluctantly Margo had to admit Seth was right—for reasons he knew nothing about. If they became lovers, and she didn't offer him a full and immediate explanation of her reason for accepting work as his housekeeper, she'd be in an untenable ethical position. Since she wasn't ready to face that hurdle, she had no business making love to him. Yet she didn't want him to go.

Meanwhile, there wasn't much doubt what would happen if they shared a bed.

"I have a guest room..." she offered uncertainly.

Seth brushed a strand of dark, curly hair back from her forehead and replaced it with a kiss. "Thanks but no thanks. I'm not willing for us to sleep that far apart."

Ultimately they compromised by dozing off right there on the couch, under a quilt Margo's grandmother had pieced together many years earlier. When they woke, stiff and groggy from sleeping scrunched together in their clothes, it was already light.

For several awkward moments, they seemed like strangers. Determined to take advantage of Sooz's absence by spending as much time with Margo as he could, Seth quickly moved to dispel the notion. Murmuring something about being creased in more places than a road map, he gave her a gentle good-morning kiss. She found the stubble of beard that had appeared on his jaw overnight intoxicating.

It was morning—time to expand the friendship part of their relationship. Slipping on his shoes, Seth volunteered to go after the Sunday paper while she put on the coffee.

Overnight, it had turned colder and started to rain. Still rumpled but relatively free of aches after exercising their necks and shoulders, they drank mugs of Margo's favorite hazelnut-flavored brew from Starbucks and ate wedges of Seth's mango cake in lieu of a more conventional breakfast.

Afterward, they spent a lazy morning passing various sections of the *Times* back and forth and mounting a joint assault on the day's crossword puzzle. Though they exchanged a few more kisses, Seth kept it light. Unless he was very much mistaken, Margo had begun to worry about what would happen when their stolen weekend had run its course. That evening, she was due to report back for work.

When it was time to part, they shared a lengthy kiss at her front door. It was soul-wrenching in its intensity.

"You needn't worry that I'll embarrass you in front of Sooz," he said when at last they came up for air. "I won't. But I have some very definite intentions where you're concerned. I don't plan to let you off the hook."

Seth had arranged to pick up Sooz from her mother around four o'clock, as the Magnusons planned to rest before attending a party that night. Returning to the house on Magnolia Boulevard a few minutes before seven, Margo got a warm but restrained welcome from Seth. Covertly squeezing her hand, he disappeared into his study. Sooz was moping at the kitchen table, trying to catch up on neglected homework.

The girl didn't respond by word or glance to Margo's greeting. "So... how was your weekend?" Margo asked with a shrug, getting out the makings of an elaborate school lunch. "Did you have a good time?"

Still Sooz refused to look at her. "It was okay, I guess," she mumbled.

Masked though it was by the noncommittal reply, Margo thought she detected a cry for help. Having learned Cheryl and her husband planned to depart for Chicago in the morning and, subsequently, to spend several months in Atlanta overseeing one of his real estate projects before passing through Seattle again on their way back to Honolulu, Margo was willing to bet she knew the reason for Sooz's distress. It was clear to anyone with half a brain that time spent with Sooz wasn't very high on the Magnusons' priority list. No dummy, the girl had easily figured it out. She was wounded to the quick.

About to ask whether Sooz had received any birthday presents she particularly liked in an effort to strike a positive note, Margo thought better of it. Kids knew the difference between money spent on them and genuine affection.

At the moment, she realized, a hug from her definitely wouldn't be appreciated.

"Know what?" she remarked, observing a strict hands-off policy. "The weather's turned cold and I could use some hot chocolate. But I hate to make it just for myself. I don't suppose I could talk you into having some..."

Early on in their acquaintance, she'd established hot chocolate as a remedy for emotional bruises and bumps. Subliminally, at least, Sooz seemed to make the connection.

"Maybe you could," the dark-eyed moppet allowed, perking up a little. "Are you any good at arithmetic?"

For the next few days, Seth didn't say or do anything to arouse Sooz's suspicions about them. Thanks to the looks they exchanged and an occasional brush of hands that seemed to come about by accident, Margo knew that it was just a temporary reprieve. Things had changed as a result of their idyllic day together and the cramped but cozy night they'd spent on her living-room couch.

In a sense, they were lovers already though they hadn't made love. Someday soon she'd have to face the music. Yet if she opted for honesty, she stood to lose the two people she cared about most.

Obviously still missing Cheryl and feeling betrayed, Sooz clung to Margo the way a drowning man might clutch at a life raft, though characteristically she made a show of maintaining her independence. In return, Margo tried to distract the girl and herself by teaching her to make clothespin angels for the Christmas tree and baking endless batches of cookies in cutout shapes, which Sooz meticulously decorated.

Margo was well aware she and Seth couldn't walk an emotional tightrope forever, pretending nothing had changed between them. Though she suffered a little stab of panic, she wasn't too surprised when, late Friday morning, he phoned from the boat yard, catching her in the midst of putting away the weekend groceries.

"I've lined up Mrs. Johnson to baby-sit," he announced. "We're going out tonight."

Just like that? What would Sooz say?

"You make it sound as if I don't have any choice," she hedged.

Living up to the horoscope Nell had cast for him, he took her cooperation for granted. "You don't," he agreed. "The Guarneri Quartet is in town and I've sprung for tickets. I refuse to let them go to waste."

Sooz was lying in the front of the television set with Bear, watching a video, when Seth got home and broke the news about their date. From her strategic vantage point in the kitchen, where she was nervously tidying up, Margo could tell the girl wasn't pleased. No doubt to her, their involvement seemed like one more rejection.

"I'm not hungry!" Sooz snapped when Margo dared to poke her head into the living room a few minutes later and offered to fix her a supper tray.

Scooping up Bear, she stomped up to her room in a blue funk. Despite her affection for Mrs. Johnson, she refused to put in an appearance when the older woman arrived.

Margo was torn with guilt. "Looks like we've done it now," she told Seth anxiously as they left the house. "We've got Sooz mad at us. And I noticed one of your next-door neighbors pulling back the curtains to observe our departure. Before you know it, our reputations will be in shreds."

Seth didn't appear perturbed as he helped her into the Mercedes' passenger seat. "To tell you the truth, I was planning to discuss that problem with you later this evening," he replied, his eyes telegraphing a message she couldn't seem to translate.

For Margo, the dinner they shared that evening at a Thai restaurant on the north shore of Green Lake and the Guarneri concert at the University of Washington that followed it, were fraught with conflicting emotions. On the one hand, she felt as if she'd re-entered the blissful, romantic state that had so captivated her the previous weekend. And on the other? Things were moving much too rapidly for comfort.

With Seth's announcement that they were "going out," she feared that Sooz had begun to view her as his new girlfriend—competition for his affection rather than a stable, caring force. Coming as it did on the heels of Cheryl's de facto abandonment, the revelation had doubtless packed a double whammy. All of Margo's efforts to win Sooz's friendship and confidence would likely be thrown back in her face.

I never should have agreed to go out with him tonight, Margo thought, thoroughly upset with herself. Sooz is the reason Seth and I got together and Sooz has to be my first priority. Yet in a man-woman way, she loved him just as much.

The weather was nippy but well above freezing. Though Margo's raincoat and zip-in liner would have been adequate protection, Seth had proposed she wear her full-length woolen coat and bring a scarf. She understood why when, as they drove out of the parking garage beneath the university's Meany Hall, he remarked that a dose of wind and salt spray aboard the Bainbridge Island ferry would be just the ticket to clear their heads.

"If you haven't ridden it before," he coaxed, "it takes just a little over an hour, round trip. The view of downtown Seattle is breathtaking."

Since it was long past rush hour and winter in the bargain, the ferry wasn't crowded. Tired shoppers and commuters, who'd stayed in town for dinner or worked late, settled back to read in the brightly lit observation salon's blue plastic chairs. The more exhausted looking stretched out on black leatherette benches by the windows.

Only the hardy opted for fresh air. Though it was cold and damp outside, Margo and Seth chose a protected spot on the rear deck, where the view would be most spectacular. As the ferry separated from the dock and they retreated from the city's brilliance, she realized fully why he'd suggested they make the trip.

The panorama that spread before them was like New York at night. Or Camelot. Taillights from a steady stream of cars glow-wormed their way over the city's hills. Its skyscrapers were bands of diamonds set in concrete. Floodlights from the Kingdome poured gold onto the hiss and slap of the water.

A light plane, winking against the overcast, passed by on the left. Nestled in Seth's arms, with tiny pinpoints of rain and mist hitting her in the face, Margo could feel the thrum of the ferry's powerful engines radiating up through the deck into the soles of her leather boots.

The further they got from it, the more unreal downtown Seattle appeared. Miniaturized, it became a toy, the scene on a glitzy postcard.

"Beautiful, isn't it?" Seth whispered.

She lifted her face to his. "I never realized . . ."

A moment later they were kissing—hungrily, desperately. Built up during a week of longing and self-denial, the force of their need for each other had grown until it was like a tornado that threatened to destroy everything in its path. Aching to succumb to its passionate intensity, Margo struggled to maintain her perspective. She couldn't help worrying about Sooz. Or the secret she'd kept from the man she loved so much.

"Seth, please!" she protested when he gave her a chance to speak. "We can't go on like this..."

"Hush, sweetheart." He placed one loving finger against her mouth. "I planned to save this for the return trip, but you've forced my hand. I know it's sudden. But I've never been more sure of anything than I am about what I feel for you. I want to marry you, Margo. Make love to you every night. In that order, so Sooz won't be scandalized and the neighbors can't disapprove."

Margo was speechless. She wasn't sure if it was the biting salt spray making her eyes water so, or if it was tears of mingled happiness and regret.

"Oh, Seth," she moaned. "You know it would never work. Sooz..."

"Hasn't been this happy since Cheryl and I divorced. Oh, I know how she behaved tonight. She's upset and jealous...probably more over me stealing you from her than vice versa. Given time, she'll learn that we can share you, and adjust. In the long run, our getting together will be the very best thing that's ever happened to her."

Unbidden, the idea that she could have Seth *and* the daughter she'd lost at birth took root in Margo's heart. The only price she'd have to pay was silence. And the loss of her self-respect. It had been one thing to riffle Seth's desk looking for a birthdate. But it would be quite another to build their marriage on a lie.

"Say yes," he prompted in a husky voice. "I love you so much."

In the end, though she confessed she loved him too, she'd only agree to think about his proposal. They were subdued, exceptionally quiet with each other as they returned to the house on Magnolia Boulevard. At Seth's invitation, Margo accompanied him upstairs to check on Sooz before leaving for the weekend. The girl was sprawled on her stomach, one arm flung out in sleep to make contact with her precious stuffed teddy.

"Cheryl gave Bear to Sooz the last Christmas we were together," Seth admitted in a hushed voice. "She hasn't been without him since."

Gazing at the stubborn, vulnerable child who had almost certainly taken shape inside her body, Margo vowed never to knowingly do anything that would hurt her. She hoped that wouldn't mean giving her up, along with the chance for a life with Seth.

The weekend, during which she'd had her father to herself, didn't improve Sooz's perspective. Returning on Sunday night, Margo found herself facing the same uphill battle that had loomed when she'd first accepted employment with Seth. No, that's not quite accurate, she thought. This is worse. Before I had a blank slate. Now Sooz views me as a traitor.

In a quiet talk with Seth one night after the girl had gone to sleep, Margo asked that he give her time. And space. She couldn't possibly go out with him—or consider discussing his marriage proposal—until the situation with Sooz smoothed out.

"If we wait until she calms down, we'll just have to go through this all over again," Seth argued, feeling her slip away. "Calling a spade a spade will force her to get used to the idea. The sooner you and I wed, the sooner all three of us will be happy together."

To his amazement, though she was usually putty in his hands, Margo wouldn't budge.

"If we can't get married right away, or even date, at the very least, I want you here on Christmas," he replied, determined to make some kind of progress with her.

Slowly she shook her head. "If I stayed, Sooz would sulk. The holiday would be miserable. Besides, I need time to think."

True to her word, Margo spent Christmas Eve alone, with her memories of Beth and Jim. But she wasn't mired in the past. Instead she was aching for Sooz and the future Seth wanted to give her. All her energy had gone into decorating the Danner household and now she was drained. She couldn't make herself put up a tree. Her effort to light a few candles and put some Christmas music on the stereo fell flat. She couldn't seem to make the holiday exist, even in her own imagination.

On Christmas Day, she dragged herself over to Nell's for dinner and found herself ducking the concern she saw in the kindly nurse-astrologer's eyes. With Nell's gentleman friend making it a threesome at the table, she managed to fend off any conversational forays into personal territory. No doubt my horoscope will get a working over tonight, she thought ruefully, returning home and taking the phone off the hook. If so, I don't want to hear about it. Or Sooz's horoscope. Or Seth's.

When she returned to work on December twenty-sixth, Sooz was so difficult it brought tears to her eyes. Maybe the best thing for everyone concerned would be for me to bow out, Margo thought. Still depressed from the holidays and afraid to tell Seth that she'd been less than honest with him, she decided to quit. Even if he could forgive me for not telling him the truth, she reasoned, he'd think I was trying to take Sooz away from him.

Meanwhile, she wants nothing to do with me. It's an impossible situation.

Seth came home to find her packing. "What are you doing?" he asked, a thunderbolt of a frown drawing his blond brows together.

When she explained that she was leaving because it would be best for all concerned, she thought he'd explode. "What happened to our six-month agreement?" he demanded angrily. "And your claim to care about us?"

Sooz chose that moment to stumble onto the tense scene. "What's going on?" she asked, looking from her father to Margo and back again with a frightened expression.

"Margo's leaving us," Seth announced in a clipped tone. "She doesn't think you want her to stay."

"Oh, but I *do*..."

Betrayed into blurting out her innermost feelings, Sooz retreated a little. But Seth wouldn't let her get by with it.

"I've asked Margo to marry me," he told the girl bluntly. "If she says yes, she'll be my wife. And your stepmother. She'll live here with us permanently. I'd appreciate it if you'd let us both know—very honestly— how you feel about that."

There was a long silence during which Sooz searched their faces, then looked down at her shoes. Appalled at the way he was handling the situation, Margo could feel Seth willing her to keep silent. The male lion at his most regal, he wouldn't welcome any interference.

"I guess ... that would be okay," the girl admitted at last.

Seth was relentless. "How about *more* than okay?"

Sooz bit her lip, then started to smile. "Yes, Daddy," she confessed.

With typical mastery, he drew them both into his arms. "Now you have to say yes," he told Margo triumphantly. "You don't have any other choice."

Chapter Seven

Stunned, Margo found herself wearing Seth's diamond. It had all happened so quickly—Sooz's capitulation, his categorical statement that now there could be no impediment to their marrying, her own surge of hope that, out of a tragic mix-up, the heartache of divorce and death and her own weak-willed failure to tell him the truth could come a happy ending for everyone. Actual belief hadn't settled in for several days.

She hadn't said yes exactly. Just nodded with tears in her eyes. Seth had kissed her and Sooz, and pronounced it a done deal. The following day, he, Margo and the energetic sprite who'd drawn them together had gone to Friedlander's to pick out an engagement ring and two wedding bands.

The diamond they'd selected was pear-shaped, nearly two carats of blue-white fire poised above a plain yellow-gold band. Their wedding rings, which matched, were also fashioned of yellow gold. For Sooz, they chose a heart-shaped gold locket set with a tiny aquamarine.

Engraved on the spot, the locket's reverse side bore the inscription *Susan, Daddy & Margo*, and the date *January 15*. Before returning it to its velvet box, Seth explained that it symbolized the important role Sooz would play in the three-way pact they'd made to love and cherish each other.

"You'll be one of the three most important people at the ceremony, pumpkin," he promised the entranced child. "When we finish exchanging wedding rings, Margo and I fasten it around your neck."

That all important moment was just eighteen days hence. Ironically, they'd chosen a date three days before the first anniversary of Beth Ann's death. Happier than she'd ever thought possible after such a wrenching loss, yet increasingly guilt-ridden as her wedding day approached, Margo wanted to believe she'd have unburdened her conscience the day they'd settled things if Sooz hadn't been standing there. But she couldn't be sure. She only knew she loved both the man and the child too much to risk losing them.

Surely love will carry us through, she told herself. Why should a secret that doesn't matter anymore be allowed to spoil things? Now that he was hers, that she knew he loved her back, life without Seth would be a desert. And though Sooz would never know the truth about their biological relationship, she'd be Margo's daughter in every practical sense.

Margo couldn't hide her qualms from Nell, who accompanied her to a well-known Sixth Avenue boutique in her search for a wedding outfit. Twisting and turning before a three-way mirror in a marked-down beauty of a pale aqua silk *duppioni* suit with pavé rhinestone buttons, she kept meeting a look that was part fondness, part worry in her friend's eyes.

"Okay...let's have it," she said, confronting Nell face-to-face.

Perched on a corner stool in the dressing room with both Margo's purse and her own, as well as several packages, piled on her lap, Nell nodded. "It's perfect...glamorous but elegant. And very flattering to your complexion."

Margo agreed. The suit was exactly what she'd been looking for. Though it was expensive even on sale, it would be worth every penny.

"You know what I mean," she countered stubbornly.

Nell sighed. "I suppose I do. You're talking about the fact that you haven't confided in Seth."

The heightened color in Margo's cheeks offered silent confirmation that the older woman was right on target.

"Since you ask, I can't help wondering if you plan to tell him about the circumstances that brought you together before saying 'I do,'" Nell admitted. "Or if you plan just to go forward, keeping the facts unearthed by those cancer researchers and the detective you hired locked away in your heart."

"You think I should tell him, don't you?" Margo said. "Don't *you*?"

Hesitating, Margo searched her own eyes in the mirror. They were bright with love and the excitement of a bride-to-be, yet they contained shadows of fear that she could lose it all.

"Half of me does," she said at last. "I hate the idea of founding our marriage on a lie...even one of omission."

"And the other half?"

"Is terrified. I let the chance to make a clean breast of things before our relationship got too hot and heavy slip away. Now I don't know what to do." Nervously she fingered one of the suit's buttons, which needed to be sewn on a bit more securely. "If I told Seth at this juncture," she added, "I'm afraid he'd lose all respect for me. All trust."

Usually so voluble with advice, most of it predicated on the stars, Nell didn't offer a peep. Though she'd almost certainly done her usual calculations, apparently, this time, Margo was on her own.

"I guess this is the one," she murmured after a moment, taking off the sleek Italian suit and replacing it on its padded hanger. "Did I tell you a dressmaker is making Sooz's gown? We couldn't find the kind of dress she wanted."

Since their marriage would be the second for them both, Margo and Seth had decided to hold it at his house, with a minister from the local Unitarian church officiating. After all, the weathered cedar, architect-designed home was big enough, and it had a sweeping view of the Sound. They couldn't ask for a more breathtaking backdrop.

The ceremony itself would be held in front of the living-room fireplace. Seth had asked his brother, Bob, to be his best man and Nell had agreed to serve as matron of honor. In her teal velvet dress, which by happenstance harmonized beautifully with Margo's suit, Sooz would be child-of-honor and flower girl.

Seth had ordered enough flowers for a cathedral. Though just twenty guests or so would be on hand to hear them speak their vows, he'd arranged a catered buffet, too, with rare roast beef, smoked salmon, petit fours and gooseberry tarts, among other delicacies.

"This is us, getting married. I want to do things right," he'd replied when Margo had objected to the cost.

At last January 15 dawned, overcast but with a good chance the sun would peek through, according to the weatherman. It was a Saturday, the last Margo was to have as a single woman in her Ravenna bungalow. Instead she opened her eyes in the charming housekeeper's suite Seth had first shown her in late October. Though she'd fully expected to go home the night before and dress for the ceremony there, her masterful Leo husband-to-be had refused to hear of it.

"We've been very careful to toe the line because of Sooz," he'd reminded her the night before, a hint of what that forbearance had cost flickering in his hazel eyes. "But, contemporary mores being what they are, I doubt most people would believe it. Since we'll be husband and wife tomorrow, what difference will it make if we spend another night sleeping apart under the same roof? I want you *here,* where I can kiss you good morning on our wedding day."

Agreeing to stay didn't give me the time and distance I needed to think, Margo moaned, burrowing deeper under the covers. I love Seth with all my heart and I want to marry him. Yet as the minutes tick by and our vows keep getting closer, it's like I'm on a speeding train, hurtling toward a mistake I'll never be able to put right.

Caught in a web of misrepresentation, though she'd never actually lied to Seth, she didn't know what to do. At this late date, bringing up the issue of Sooz's parentage and the way she'd deceived him was almost unthinkable. Yet she found herself longing to do just that. I should have told him everything months ago, she thought miserably. The day we met at the boat yard, I should have been right up-front.

You know what would have happened, her pragmatic self replied. He'd have been upset. And angry. The two of you would have ended up on the opposite sides of a very high fence.

Just then there was a light knock on her bedroom door. Seth eased it open. Dressed in old jeans and a plaid flannel shirt that made him look like a redheaded lumberjack, he was balancing a tray loaded with coffee, a basket of bakery shop goodies and a bud vase containing a single mum. There were even a place mat and two carefully folded cloth napkins.

"Wake up, sleepyhead," he exhorted, putting the tray down on the coverlet beside her and leaning over to give her a possessive kiss. "The caterers and the florist will be here sooner than you think. And Sooz is jumping out of her skin. You can't stay in bed forever if you expect to snag a scapegrace stepdaughter and a thoroughly besotted husband."

Reluctantly Margo pulled herself up against the bed pillows. "Oh, Seth . . ."

It was an unmistakable wail of uncertainty, seeking comfort. Plopping down on the end of the bed, Seth grinned and reached under the covers. "What's the matter?" he teased. "Cold feet? Let me warm them up for you."

"Seth, don't! You're going to spill . . ."

"No, I'm not. Just tickle the bride-to-be."

Margo was *very* ticklish. "No...no! Please stop!" she begged, letting out a squeal of dismay.

"Daddy, you're sloshing coffee on the napkins," Sooz reproved from the doorway, where she'd plainly been lying in wait for the opportunity to make an entrance. A moment later, she'd dissolved in giggles and joined the fray.

Following Margo's unconditional surrender, the three of them munched doughnuts and other assorted breakfast treats on her bed. Clearly thrilled to be in the center of things, Sooz hadn't uttered a single complaint about the prospect of staying behind in Mrs. Johnson's care while her father and Margo honeymooned in San Francisco. Meanwhile Seth was eyeing Margo as if he'd rather take a bite out of her than his favorite honey-dipped crullers. What more could a woman want?

This may not be anyone else's version of heaven, but it's certainly mine, Margo thought. The question was, did she deserve it? Like the runaway train she'd pictured, time seemed to be speeding up, making it more and more difficult for her to set the record straight.

Soon, much too soon, Sooz was offering to carry the breakfast tray back downstairs and Seth was dialing the airlines to check on their flight reservations. It was time for Margo to get up, shower, dress in jeans herself, and plunge into last-minute preparations.

They'd decided on a late afternoon wedding. Getting everything ready would be quite a task and Nell came over early to help. Her stomach queasy with guilt, Margo didn't have an uninterrupted moment to talk with Seth. Though he was prowling about, supervising their efforts and doing his best to pitch in, Sooz, Nell, or someone else, like the florist, always seemed to be underfoot.

Nell's expression was pleased but guarded. By contrast, Seth was pleasantly wired. Sooz bubbled over with excitement and self-importance. When the caterers arrived, she started issuing orders to them like a miniature martinet.

Before they knew it, the hours had fled and it was time to dress. Leaving Nell in charge, they went upstairs—Seth to his room and Margo to Sooz's, where she helped the girl put on brand new, frilly underwear and her teal velvet dress. Though Sooz's hair wasn't quite as curly as Margo's, it coaxed easily into ringlets. Her legs were skinny, coltish in the white tights they'd chosen to go with her black patent Mary-Janes.

Sooz is growing up fast, Margo realized. Her childhood's almost half over. She didn't want to do anything that would cause them to be separated again.

"You look gorgeous, honey," she said with a lump in her throat.

"Do I really?" Sooz preened in front of the mirror over her dresser, then turned to give Margo one of her rare, spontaneous hugs. "Now you," she prodded. "Daddy said we should get a move on."

Their guests would begin arriving in less than three-quarters of an hour. Clinging to her like a limpet, Sooz followed Margo into her suite.

"I wish you had a train and a veil," she chattered when Margo emerged from her private bath in a lacy bra, bikini pants and matching garter belt to draw on sheer hose and slip into her chic Italian suit. "You should have let *me* pick out your dress. It would have been white, with a long, long train. I'm going to wear white when I get married someday. And have a great big wedding cake, with a little bride and groom on top and lots of layers and roses made of frosting."

As the girl rattled on, Margo could feel her crisis of conscience coming to a head. Could she make it through the ceremony without first telling Seth the truth? The closer their nuptials came, the more it looked as if the answer had to be no.

The doorbell rang and guests began arriving as she put on her makeup, Sooz in rapt attendance. A buzz of festive talk quickly filled the house. Margo recognized the voices of Bob and Joy Danner, as well as that of a good friend she'd worked with during her hospital public relations days. What would they think, she tormented herself, if I broke down and confessed the truth in the middle of the ceremony?

"You look kind of funny," Sooz observed, pausing in the midst of her monologue. "Are you okay? Mrs. Johnson says..."

For some reason, Sooz's awareness of the war that was raging inside her pushed Margo to the breaking point. "Sooz, honey, please go get your daddy and tell him I have to talk to him," she said in an anguished voice.

"You can't," the girl replied matter-of-factly. "Once you're dressed, he's not supposed to see you until you come down the stairs with your bouquet."

It was now or never. And, though they were hanging on by their fingernails, Margo's scruples had won the fight. "I *have* to, sweetheart," she begged. "Please..."

Something in her tone worried Sooz into obedience. With a backward glance at Margo, the girl ran off. Seth appeared a minute later, strikingly handsome in a dark gray business suit with a carnation in his lapel.

Before Margo could say anything, he enfolded her. God but he smelled good—like soap and shaving cream, his own special blend of skin scent and after-shave. He *felt* good, too. All warmth and reassurance. It was like having the world in her arms. If she lost him and Sooz, her life wouldn't be worth a damn.

"You're so lovely," he whispered, kissing her and then drawing back a little to repair her smudged lipstick with one gentle fingertip. "I forbid you to get cold feet again. Our guests will be convinced I'm torturing you if I have to reapply the tickle treatment. We don't want them to call the police."

Margo didn't laugh, or crack a smile. She felt sick all over. "I'm not getting cold feet," she said, drowning in the love she saw in his eyes and hoping it would still be there when she'd finished. "But you might... after you hear what I have to say."

He smoothed her cheek. "Isn't it a little late to reveal you already have a husband somewhere? Or that you're wanted for bigamy in three states?"

Resolute, she forged ahead. "This is serious, Seth."

Something really *was* the matter. He started paying attention. "All right, cupcake," he said. "I'm listening."

Now that she had his ear, Margo didn't know where to start. There didn't seem to be any choice but to meet the issue head-on. "Before we get married, there's something I think you should know," she told him. "I didn't lie to you. But I took the housekeeping job with you under false pretenses."

Seth frowned in disbelief. Was she flipping out, out of nervousness? "*What* false pretenses?" he demanded skeptically. "I didn't check out your references with the hospital where you used to work, but I'm sure they were first-rate. Your homemaking skills are everything an employer could want, though at this point I wouldn't care if you couldn't boil water. Best of all, you've charmed Sooz out of her emotional suit of armor and made me come alive again. So what's left to worry about?"

A *lot* was left. Margo chose her words with care. "When I called about your ad in the paper," she said, "it was because I wanted to find out more about Sooz, not because I was looking for a housekeeping position."

Confusion and bafflement registered on Seth's face. "I don't get it," he confessed. "You'd never met either of us before. Why on earth...?"

"It's a long story." Her words halting and painful, Margo described the rarity of Jim's cancer, Beth's tissue testing as part of a national research program and the mind-bending results.

His puzzlement only deepened. "No doubt you should have told me about this before," he admitted. "After all, we're about to be married and I have a right to know if something's bothering you. But I don't see how this changes anything. You mentioned when I hired you that you missed your daughter, and liked the idea of being around another child."

"Not just another child. Sooz. You see, after I got over the shock that Beth wasn't Jim's and my biological child, I realized that the baby I'd carried for nine months had to be out there in the world somewhere. I became convinced she and Beth had been switched inadvertently. I had to find her."

"And you think that Sooz... Margo, that just doesn't make sense! So what if your child and mine would have been the same age? There are thousands of female children born in Seattle every year."

Having begun, Margo had to follow through. "I know how this must sound...today of all days," she said. "But I didn't fasten on Sooz out of thin air. When the hospital refused to give me any information because of privacy statutes and the understandable fear that a lawsuit might result, I hired a detective. I don't know how he found out, but he got back to me with the news that there were only two female Caucasian babies in the Bayless Memorial nursery at the time our Beth Ann was there...Beth and Sooz."

Crazy as Margo's story about tissue tests and inadvertent baby-swapping sounded, it was plausible, Seth supposed. But to hint that Sooz might be her missing child was completely outlandish. Much as he loved her, Seth began to wonder if pre-wedding jitters had caused Margo's mind to snap.

Yet as she talked about hospital records and hammered home details, he began to realize her astonishing tale wasn't fantasy, at least in her own head. She'd actually set out to deceive him!

"So you answered my ad to do a little investigating of your own, is that it?" he asked, the Leo temper she hadn't glimpsed before putting in an appearance at last.

Terrified he'd reject her, Margo nodded. "I had to find out for myself, don't you see?"

It was all true—the tissue test on her daughter and the detective she'd hired. Her bald-faced masquerade. Well, he'd be damned if he'd accept the conclusion she'd drawn. Sooz was his child, his flesh and blood! She had absolutely no right...

Furious, he grabbed Margo by the shoulders, his strong fingers biting into her flesh through her suit's rich fabric. "Exactly what did you have in mind?" he demanded cuttingly. "Taking Sooz away from me if she came up to snuff? Or would you have settled for visitation rights? Did you plan to drag me and my ex-wife into court?"

Caught in his remorseless grip, Margo fought back tears. She wanted him to forgive her, not hate her. "I'm not sure what I thought would happen," she confessed, aching to rest her head against his chest. "I just wanted to make certain she was well cared for. And loved."

"How noble, given your methods! Too bad your scheming didn't stop there!" By now, Seth was shouting. He wanted to shake her. Instead he dropped his hands, clenching them at his sides.

"I don't know what you mean," Margo protested, her desperation escalating a notch. "I fell in love with you..."

"Like hell you did. You only pretended to, in your obsession to get at Sooz. What a coup it must have been when I asked you to marry me! You had me so hooked you could keep me dangling while you thought it over. I have to hand it to you, lady... you deserve an Academy Award for your whole damn performance!"

His pride had been hurt. He felt threatened and humiliated. Margo didn't need the astrological chart Nell had drawn up for him to realize she was in dangerous emotional territory. He was like a big, wounded lion, ready to go for the jugular.

"I wasn't honest with you," she admitted. "And I'm very, very sorry about that. But you've got to believe me when I say I love you"

"I don't have to believe any such thing."

Announcing her presence with a discreet tap, Nell poked her head in the door. "Sorry to interrupt," she murmured apologetically. "But your voices are carrying."

Though Seth quieted in a heartbeat, his anger became even more terrible. His friends were whispering about him. He'd have to face them and admit he'd made a mistake. As for his little girl, she'd be devastated. She might never trust anyone again.

"Seth, please..." Margo begged. "Forgive me..."

The entreaty didn't seem to register.

"Stay here," he ordered, his firmly hewn features as implacable as granite. "I'm going downstairs and call the whole thing off. Once everyone leaves, Sooz and I are going out. We won't be back for several hours. I want you *gone* by the time we return."

Chapter Eight

On the verge of collapse, Margo watched helplessly as Seth brushed past her friend on his way out. "Oh, Nell," she whispered. "I've lost them..."

Without a word, the older woman enfolded her. For a moment, they held fast to each other, Nell rocking her as if she were an injured child.

Then, "Come sit down...you're shivering," Nell urged, guiding her to the padded window seat of the pleasant sitting room she'd planned to turn into a sewing and craft area for herself and Sooz.

She was still wearing her beautiful Italian suit. But what did it matter now if the delicate silk fabric got wrinkled and crushed? There wouldn't be a wedding. Or a soul-consuming nuptial kiss. The photographs a friend of Seth's had planned to shoot would never be taken.

Like a whipped dog that wants only to retreat from the world and lick its wounds, Margo curled up under the quilt Nell spread over her lap. Taking a seat beside her,

Nell drew Margo's head against her shoulder. "I'm so *sorry,* hon," she commiserated.

"We were perfect for each other, Nell."

"I know you were. You still are, dearest girl. His pride's hurt, that's all. Nobody likes being deceived by someone they love. Given time..."

"No. It's hopeless. Even if Seth could forgive me, he'd want to protect Sooz. He's convinced...that I never cared about him. In his mind, all I really wanted was...was...to take her away from him."

Her heart aching at the thought of what their change in plans would do the dark-haired moppet she'd almost certainly carried beneath her heart, Margo burst into tears. Emotionally abandoned by Cheryl, Sooz had blossomed under her care, despite an occasionally difficult period of adjustment. Once Sooz had conceded it would be "more than okay" for Margo and her father to get married, she'd seemed pleased and excited at the prospect.

Now those plans were shattered. It would be doubly difficult for Sooz to trust anyone again. I wonder what Seth's going to tell her, Margo agonized. The whole story? Or just that it's over between us? I hope I haven't hurt her too much.

From downstairs, she could hear the terse rumble of Seth's voice as he spoke to their guests, though she couldn't make out his words. Shocked murmurs and what were probably embarrassed condolences were followed by a general exodus, the syncopated slamming of car doors. Margo pictured Sooz crying, Mrs. Johnson comforting her.

When at last the house was quiet, and all the guests had gone, Seth returned for a moment. Though to all outward appearances he was in control, his gaze drilled into Margo's with a multitude of accusations.

"The coast is clear," he announced in a clipped tone, ignoring Nell. "When I said I wanted you gone, I meant you *and* your possessions. There'll be no coming back for something you deliberately forgot."

He hopes to erase me from his life as if I never existed, Margo thought. All the love I felt has turned to hate. "Is . . . Sooz okay?" she summoned the courage to ask.

Briefly the full power of Seth's fury showed itself. "Sooz isn't your concern," he ground out. "You're not to go near her again."

Her heart aching, Margo watched silently as Seth turned his back to her and walked away. Though she knew it would be a form of self-torture, she threw off the quilt and ran to her bedroom window, which overlooked the drive. She was just in time to watch as Seth led Sooz out to the Mercedes. The girl was still wearing her teal velvet dress and white tights. Because the day was chilly, Seth had seen to it that she'd put on her winter coat.

Margo caught only a glimpse of Sooz's face. Yet she could read intense hurt and bewilderment there. The last shred of her self-esteem withering, she buried her face in her hands.

Nell had come to stand behind her. As Seth backed the Mercedes out to the street and headed east toward the Garfield Street overpass at a high rate of speed, she rested a hand on Margo's shoulder. "I can imagine how you must feel," she said softly. "But maybe we'd better do as he says."

If she failed to vacate the premises as ordered, Margo believed Seth was capable of calling the police. He was *that* angry with her. "Okay," she responded numbly, turning away from the window. "I don't have any packing boxes. We'll have to stuff most of my junk in your station wagon as is, if that's all right."

Functioning as if in a self-induced trance, Margo changed to jeans and an old sweater and started gathering her possessions together. But her seeming calm was a fragile one. As she and Nell descended the stairs with the first load, the reality of what had happened struck her afresh. More tears streamed down her face.

The wedding flowers Seth had ordered, so riotous in their profusion, had taken on a funereal air. Untouched and suddenly nauseating in its perfection, the lavish buffet their guests were to have enjoyed seemed to mock her. Apparently Seth had sent the white-coated waiters home. For all he cared, she supposed, the food could rot.

Aware that some of the neighbors had been invited guests and were probably watching her, Margo stowed her things in Nell's station wagon and her convertible as quickly as possible.

"That's it, I guess," Nell said at last. "Unless you've got stuff to load up from the kitchen, too."

Margo shook her head. "Nothing that matters. But there *is* something I have to do before I leave."

She'd thought of writing Seth a note. But there wasn't anything she could say that he hadn't heard already. If he was going to come around, he'd have to do it on his own. She doubted it would ever happen. When he'd ordered her out of his house, it had been goodbye in no uncertain terms.

Remembering all too well the morning she'd riffled his desk in search of his birthdate so Nell could cast his horoscope, Margo slipped into Seth's office. Their plane tickets to San Francisco were lying on his blotter. Touching them lightly, lingeringly, as if they were mementos of a long-lost love, she opened a side drawer and took out a plain, business-size envelope. Though every instinct in her cried out against it, she slowly drew Seth's diamond off her finger and dropped it inside, sealing the flap. Placing the envelope beside the airline tickets, she left the room without a backward look.

Somehow she managed to hold herself together sufficiently to drive as she followed Nell's well-traveled Volvo back to her Ravenna bungalow, which she'd planned to rent out after the honeymoon. But once she got there, she wasn't up to putting her things away in their proper places.

"Just leave everything in the hall," she told Nell despairingly. "I'll take care of it later. Right now, I . . ."

"Need to sit down and catch your breath."

Putting one arm about Margo's shoulders, Nell led her to the tulip-printed couch where she and Seth had spent the night. Though Margo had dared to dream otherwise, that night would be the only one she'd ever spend in his arms. If there was a bottomless pit in the world, she'd found it.

"After what happened, I feel a little shaky, too," Nell confessed. "I'll fix us each a drink."

There was a little cognac left in the bottle. Dividing it between two small glasses, Nell returned to Margo's side and handed one of them to her.

"I should have known better," Margo said, accepting it. "Keeping Seth in the dark about the way our daughters were switched was wrong. So was getting romantically involved with him. But if I hadn't done the former, the latter wouldn't have happened. And I do love him so."

Nell was silent a moment. "To be honest, I was afraid something like this would happen," she admitted as

Margo forced herself to take a sip of the fiery amber liquid. "I saw trouble in your horoscope from the day you met him."

Margo raised a tear-stained face. "Why didn't you say something?"

"Ah, hon..." Helplessly Nell patted her shoulder. "You were pretty determined. You didn't want to be told. Besides... though the stars are usually right about the traps we set for ourselves, I hoped... well, that this time they were mistaken."

In a downtown restaurant, Seth was trying to explain things to Sooz. The story he'd concocted—that he'd found out Margo wasn't such a nice person after all and decided not to marry her—didn't satisfy his daughter. To his chagrin, she demanded details.

"What did she *do,* Daddy? Was it something really bad?" the girl asked, obviously confused and frightened by the afternoon's events.

Heartsick over what the breakup was doing to his child, and unable to reveal the root cause of his anger without divulging Margo's stunning allegations, he repeated lamely that the marriage would never have worked.

In response, Sooz fiddled with her knife and fork. Always quick to note when one of her questions wasn't getting a direct answer, she appeared to be thinking things over. "You won't ever get mad at *me* like that, will you?" she queried after a moment, darting him a look.

"No, never!" Stung, Seth grasped Sooz's hands in his much bigger ones and held them tightly. "I promise, pumpkin. You'll always be my little girl. Nobody and nothing is ever going to change that."

Because of the amazing story Margo had told him, the words had a hollow ring. Worries over what she might try to do drifted through his head on the way home. As ordered, the space where she'd usually parked the M.G. was empty. He knew without having to look that her sitting room would be stripped bare of the plants, framed photographs and hand-woven toss pillows that had lent it such a comfortable air. The rest of the house, which she'd begun to decorate, wouldn't have changed, but it would be empty of her.

Incredibly he *missed* her. And hated himself for it.

I'll be damned if I'll forgive her . . . take her back, he thought, longing to slam his fist through the windshield. All she wants is Sooz. I was just a means to an end.

Before the gossip over their aborted wedding quieted down, there'd probably be a new and even more sensational rumor making the rounds. Once Margo recovered her equilibrium, she'd probably serve him with a court summons. He'd find himself fighting for his own child's custody!

To be fair, he'd have to tell Cheryl about the situation. As Sooz's mother, she had a right to know. Yet he shrank from the humiliation it would entail. Gritting his teeth, he promised himself to call her right away.

His insides eaten up with anger, dread and embarrassment, he walked into the house to face spoiling food, a semicircle of empty folding chairs and the travesty of floral decorations. Though ethically she'd been right to leave it, the white envelope he discovered on his desktop a few minutes later turned out to be the most telling blow of all. Tumbling out into his palm when he tore the envelope open, the beautiful, pear-shaped diamond he'd placed on Margo's engagement finger symbolized love turned to ashes. Seth had never been the sort of man to cry easily. Yet as he consigned the ring to the bottom of a desk drawer until he could return it to the jeweler's where he'd purchased it, he was very near tears.

Alone in her quiet bungalow after Nell left, Margo holed up in bed to cry her eyes out and live on ice cream and potato chips. After a week of misery, she couldn't take it any longer. I don't have any claim on Seth, she thought. But Sooz is my child. I have to make sure she's all right.

She didn't dare go near the house. Seth would have her arrested. But maybe if she drove over to Sooz's school…

Putting on a scarf and dark glasses in the hope she wouldn't be recognized, she drove over to the Magnolia section of town and parked a half block from the school grounds. The day was chilly and she huddled inside her turned-up coat collar as she waited for recess to start.

Sooz's school, Blaine Elementary, was situated cater-cornered to the hardware store, behind a tall chain-link fence and velvety green playing field. The beige-and-brown brick building, with its prominent gym, was set among tall deciduous trees.

Suddenly a buzzer rang. A blue-painted door nestled between the gym and a classroom wing burst open. Children poured forth, their bright parkas and scarves and mittens dancing like leaves in an autumn wind.

Uncertain what she'd say if she and Sooz came face-to-face, Margo got out of her convertible and crossed the street. Standing beside a tree trunk close to the fence, she searched the crowd of darting, laughing youngsters for the strong-willed, outspoken little girl she'd come to love.

Her heart skipped a beat as she caught sight of a familiar yellow beret and white quilted winter jacket, skinny legs encased in flowered tights. It was Sooz.

At the same moment, the girl saw her. Plainly recognizing Margo despite her attempt to appear inconspicuous, Sooz took several steps in her direction, then hesitated. Moments later, she'd turned her back and surrounded herself with her classmates as if for protection.

When Seth came home that night, Sooz was seated quietly in front of the unlit living-room fireplace, with Bear hugged tightly to her chest. She didn't move as he gave Mrs. Johnson cab fare and wished her good-night.

"Okay, baby doll...what's up?" he asked, sitting down beside her. "Did something go wrong at school?"

Sooz squirmed a little. "I, uh, saw Margo today."

Seth felt as if he'd been punched in the stomach. Simultaneously, his anger flared. "When and where did this happen?" he demanded.

"At recess. She was standing by the edge of the playground, outside the fence."

He winced, imagining the scene. It was starting already. "You didn't talk to her, I hope?"

"No. I didn't think you'd want me to."

"You were right, honey."

Sooz was silent a moment. "Daddy, why did you and Margo break up? Is she really a bad person?"

He'd never be able to tell her the truth. If she found out, it would give her nightmares. As for the heartache...

"Ah, cupcake." Seth hugged her close. "The reasons Margo and I called it quits are a bit too complicated for a nine-year-old to understand. Just trust me when I say it never would have worked. We're better off apart."

Though deep down Seth was grieving over the death of his relationship with the petite, dark-haired woman he'd grown to love, consciously he'd managed to convince himself that everything he'd felt for her had been a lie. He refused even to question whether Margo's story about an inadvertent baby swap might be true.

If it is, I don't want to know, he thought the following afternoon as he rode the elevator up to his attorney's office on the fifty-eighth floor of the Columbia Center building. And I'm damn well going to see to it she doesn't traumatize Sooz, or disrupt our lives again.

Though her heart wasn't in it, Margo was at her computer, churning out copy for an orthodontist's patient newsletter, when her doorbell rang. She didn't recognize the slight, balding man who waited diffidently for her to answer.

"Yes?" she inquired.

"Mrs. Margo Rourke?"

She nodded.

"Court order for you, ma'am." He handed her a flat, white envelope. "Have a nice day."

Was somebody *suing* her? Shutting her front door against the damp chill of a late January day, she tore the envelope open. To her astonishment, it contained a restraining order. Seth had gone before a judge to prevent her from attempting to see Sooz or contact her again. Apparently that included watching the girl through a playground fence.

Devastated, she sunk into one corner of her livingroom couch with the court document on her lap and tried to think. Up to now, she'd rejected the idea of using legal means to determine if Sooz was her daughter. In part, that was because she hadn't wanted to upset the girl further. She'd also secretly continued to hope Seth might have second thoughts.

Now she knew he wouldn't. Instead he'd drawn up battle lines. He didn't appear to care whether or not her story had any validity. Or consider how he might have reacted if their situations had been reversed. Much as she loved him, she couldn't ignore the painful knot of anger and hurt that had formed in the pit of her stomach.

It was Nell's day off. Bent on taking some kind of action, she went to the phone and dialed the older woman's number. "Seth's filed a restraining order to keep me away from Sooz," she announced when Nell answered. "All I did was go over to her school and look at her through the playground fence. I don't think I can stand to live the rest of my life not knowing whether I gave birth to her. If I sued to compel a blood test, with tissue testing to follow if researchers believed it was warranted..."

"Hon, I'm not so sure that's a good idea," Nell cautioned. "At the moment, your stars point toward maintaining a low profile. If you gave Seth a chance..."

Regretful on the day she and Seth had parted company that Nell hadn't been more forthcoming with her advice, Margo was no longer in any mood to listen. "He's had plenty of time to think and this court order is the result," she replied, her determination crystallizing. "If I'm ever to know the truth, I've got to go ahead."

Tom McMillan, the attorney who'd negotiated damages for Margo following Beth Ann's death in the school bus accident, had an office in the Columbia Center building, too. Though at first he appeared to find her tale of switched infants a bit farfetched, the letters and accompanying documentation she'd received from research scientists involved in the cancer-heredity project seemed to impress him. So did the meticulously written report compiled by Harry Spence.

"You may actually have something here, Mrs. Rourke," he admitted at last. "Though the odds are against something like this occurring, it seems to be within the realm of possibility. I happen to know Jake Nauman, Seth Danner's attorney, rather well. If you like, I'll give him a call. Maybe we can avoid the expense and heartache of pursuing legal channels on this."

Though she was willing to bet any attempt to negotiate with Seth would be doomed to failure, Margo agreed that Tom McMillan should give it a try. She wasn't surprised when, at Seth's insistence, his attorney refused even to discuss the situation.

"We'll have to file a lawsuit if you wish to proceed," Tom informed her after he'd phoned. "It's going to be costly, both in financial and emotional terms."

Seth's refusal to discuss things only solidified Margo's position. "I don't want to hurt Susan Danner," she said. "But if, as I suspect, she's my biological child, I have a right to know. We both have a right to some kind of relationship based on that unalterable truth."

A clerk from her attorney's law firm filed the lawsuit twenty-four hours later. Almost immediately, reporters got wind of it. They started digging for the identity of the child involved, though the judge assigned to the case had sealed the court records for Sooz's protection.

All they had initially was Margo's name, and she wouldn't talk to them. Learning from birth records at the King County Courthouse that Seth had a daughter born on the same day in the same hospital as her deceased child, they started dogging him with questions and struck a nerve. Ejecting them from the boatworks after threat-

ening to call the authorities, Seth found more news-
hounds camped out on either side of his drive when he
returned home that night. Promising they'd shield Sooz's
identity from public knowledge, they pleaded to interview her and Seth.

As he brushed them rudely aside and vanished into the
house, his fury at Margo knew no bounds. He'd have her
hide for this if it was the last thing he ever did! Yet in one
way he knew he was partly to blame for it. If he hadn't
filed the restraining order, maybe Margo would have
looked but not touched and left well enough alone.

Whatever the case, the hostilities had escalated.
Though he had no intention of speaking to the press on
the subject *ever,* he'd have to talk to Sooz. Reporters had
already guessed her identity. If Margo's suit wasn't
thrown out of court, eventually the story would surface
in the media. Before that happened, Sooz needed to hear
the details from him. That way, if her name and photograph appeared on television or in the papers, and the
case was bandied about at school, she wouldn't be caught
off guard, or hurt quite as much.

"Sooz, honey...come here and sit by me," he said,
after warning Mrs. Johnson not to speak with anyone
and seeing her to her cab. "We need to have a little chat."

Something in his tone seemed to alert Sooz that their
discussion would be a serious one. "What is it, Daddy?"
she asked, her dark eyes somber and brimming with
questions as she nestled in his lap.

He didn't know where to start. How in the hell was he
supposed to make a nine-year-old understand what was
happening without scaring her half to death? *I'll never
forgive Margo for doing this to us,* he thought as he
hugged Sooz close.

"Margo has a funny idea that you're really *her* little girl, not mine," he said, forcing himself to proceed. "She thinks you and her daughter... the one who died... got mixed up when you were both babies in the Bayless Memorial Hospital nursery."

Sooz flinched. "No! That's wrong," she cried. "I've *always* been your little girl. You're my daddy..."

Seth wanted to weep. Or shout. At the very least to gnash his teeth. "Of course you have," he reassured with barely controlled anguish, smoothing Sooz's hair. "And you always *will* be. This is just a crazy idea Margo has. Unfortunately, she's asked a judge to look into it. Nothing's going to happen as result of that, but people might find out and ask a lot of questions. I only told you so you'd know if anybody mentioned it."

Clearly frightened by allegations she didn't comprehend, Sooz burrowed against him. "Margo really *is* a bad person," she decided. "She won't come and try to take me away from you, will she?"

In Seth's opinion, that was exactly what Margo had in mind. "Never," he vowed. "I promise, sweetheart... I won't let her do any such thing."

In the morning, Jake Nauman talked reason to him. "If we let this case go to trial, your daughter's the one who'll be hurt most by it," the attorney counseled. "I know at this point it goes against the grain. But I think we should meet with Mrs. Rourke and her attorney. I know McMillan well, and he's a reasonable man. Maybe we can work something out."

At the mention of a possible compromise, Seth's redheaded Leo temper got the best of him. "I don't want to see Margo Rourke!" he hurled back. "*Or* to work things out with her. There's absolutely nothing to discuss. Sooz is my daughter, and that's all there is to it."

A tall, thin man in his early sixties with a calm demeanor, Jake Nauman rested a hand on Seth's arm in an appeal for moderation. "It's my advice that we don't cut off our nose to spite our face in this matter," he said. "We'll never know how much ground there is to be gained until we try. What do you say we set up a meeting for sometime later this week?"

It would be painful beyond belief being in the same room with Margo, let alone discussing whether she had a right to Sooz. Yet maybe Jake was right. If he could get the monkey of her lawsuit off his back, facing her would be worth it. Though Seth continued to glower, he didn't object.

Interpreting his silence as a concession, Jake consulted his calendar. "Let's say Thursday," he proposed. "Here in my office, at 2:00 p.m. I expect you to let me do most of the talking."

Chapter Nine

Margo got off the elevator at the Columbia Center's fifty-eighth floor with trepidation. A scant ten minutes early, she half expected to find Seth pacing there. Instead the plush reception area of Nauman, Gainsborough and Knight, Attorneys at Law, was empty except for a receptionist seated behind a semi-circular cherrywood desk.

"I'm Mrs. Rourke," Margo said, nervously clutching the strap of her shoulder bag. "I'm supposed to meet my attorney, Tom McMillan, here..."

"Ah, yes." The woman smiled pleasantly, no curiosity in sight, as if the firm handled baby-swap cases every day. "Mr. McMillan hasn't arrived yet. If you'd care to wait?"

I'd rather be boiled in oil, Margo thought, wishing now that she'd taken Nell's advice and given Seth a little more leeway. Yet she was convinced nothing would have been gained by it. Since she'd confessed the truth about her motives, the situation between them had gone from bad to worse.

Without replying, she walked over to a sweeping expanse of plate-glass windows that overlooked downtown Seattle. Out in Elliott Bay, a ferry chugged toward Bainbridge Island, trailing its miniature wake. Matchbox cars and buses plied the streets between jutting skyscrapers, which arose from their matrix of lower buildings like some exotic form of vegetation, a breathtaking study in smoked glass and concrete. There was the Mutual Bank Tower, there the First Interstate Center. Was it possible that, so high above the city, a saner perspective could be achieved?

She was startled by a light touch on her shoulder. Tom McMillan had joined her. "Hi," she said in a small voice. "I'm half sick to my stomach."

He squeezed her hand reassuringly. "Before we go in, I'd like you to think about something. Your former fiancé has been Susan's father since the nursery identification card printed with the words Baby Girl Danner was first attached to her crib. Whether or not he sired her, his emotional attachment to her must be tremendous."

Margo shook her head. "I realize that. But..."

"Right now, I'm willing to bet his greatest fear is that you'll try to take her away from him. If that isn't your objective, we might be able to convince him to allow the tests you want provided you agree not to seek custody."

"You mean...give her up in advance? Even if she turns out to be my baby?"

"Not entirely. Visitation would still be a possibility if Susan didn't object..."

The receptionist was motioning to them. "Mr. Nauman is ready to see you now."

Tom McMillan nodded. "Think about it, Margo," he said. "It could save everyone a lot of heartache."

Ironically, the room Jake Nauman had chosen for their discussion overlooked Pill Hill and the hospital where both Sooz and Beth had been born. Seth was seated beside his lawyer at a rectangular conference table, his back to the windows. Giving Margo a brief, flinty look, he stared down at his hands.

Pleasant but a bit austere, Jack Nauman welcomed them. Tom's response matched his, with perhaps a shade more warmth. Margo's was barely audible. For his part, Seth didn't say a word.

God but he's wonderful, Margo thought, unable to keep her eyes off the man she'd almost married and still loved. She longed to circumvent the expanse of polished wood that stretched like a mine field between them and throw herself into his arms.

To a degree she hadn't thought possible, she'd forgotten just how big, muscular and sexy Seth was. His red-gold hair was slightly mussed, as if he'd recently raked his fingers through it. His blond brows and lashes, features she'd doted on from the first, offered a disarmingly boyish contrast to the tightly clenched, furious man he'd become.

"Well, then," said Jake, glancing around the table. "Where shall we start?"

Margo's attorney aligned the pen and legal pad he'd taken from his briefcase before answering. "It's our hope that by meeting this way, we can spare the court and both parties a great deal of time and expense," he replied. "Since you and Mr. Danner have both had ample time to review your copies of the research scientists' findings and the highly suggestive report compiled by detective Harry Spence, I'm sure you'll agree there's sufficient evidence for a judge to look into the matter. Why not permit Susan Danner to undergo a simple blood test as part of a school physical or routine checkup? If it turns out to be negative, you've heard the last of us. No more lawsuit, uncertainty or heartache.''

Thoughtfully Jake stroked his jaw. "And if it's positive? Mind you, I don't expect it to be. But supposing it is?"

"Then I would think both Mrs. Rourke and Mr. Danner would want the confirmation or denial of a genetic tissue test . . .''

"The hell I would!" Shrugging off Jake's restraining hand on his arm, Seth leaped to his feet. "Sooz is my daughter, not Mrs. Rourke's . . . no matter what a bunch of researchers say! I'll leave town . . . abandon my home, my business and vanish before I hand her over to a conniving, dishonest stranger!''

Another second and he'd be out the door. Tom threw Margo an urgent look. *Say something,* he advised silently. Or we'll have a long, acrimonious fight ahead.

The word *stranger* had twisted like a knife in Margo's gut. Oh, Seth, she grieved. Whatever else I am, I'm not that. If I hadn't broken down and told you the truth, we'd be sharing a life. And a bed. Our little girl . . .

"Is Sooz all right?" she asked tremulously, the question coming straight from her heart.

For a moment Seth appeared nonplussed. Then, "She's fine," he snapped, grudgingly resuming his chair. "She wants nothing to do with you."

Silence reigned as Margo absorbed the blow. Even if I'm right and we win in court, I've lost them, she realized. But I've still got to know the truth. Leaning over, she whispered something in her attorney's ear.

Nodding several times, Tom gave her an approving look. "My client has just instructed me to offer a compromised proposal," he announced, glancing from Jake to Seth and back again. "If Mr. Danner will allow the necessary genetic testing to determine biological relationships in this case, she'll drop her suit and agree not to seek custody...even if the child known as Susan Danner turns out to be her natural daughter."

Jake and Seth exchanged a look. Astonishment and something else—regret at his estrangement from the petite, dark-haired woman seated across the table from him, perhaps?—flickered in Seth's eyes.

"Further," Tom continued, forestalling what Margo guessed would be their next question, "she'll be guided in any attempt to secure visitation rights by Susan Danner's wishes and the advice of a mutually agreed upon psychiatrist. Given the facts, I can't imagine any more fair or reasonable position she could take."

Jake Nauman clearly wasn't the sort of attorney to shoot from the hip. Or attempt to persuade a client of Seth's obvious temperament in front of the opposition. "If you'll give me and Mr. Danner a moment to confer in private," he murmured, "we'll get right back to you."

Giving Margo a sidelong glance that didn't reveal his thoughts, Seth followed his attorney from the room.

"That was a wise move," Tom complimented her when they were out of earshot. "In actions of this sort involving highly charged emotions on both sides, sometimes a Pyrrhic victory is worse than no victory at all. If Susan turns out to be your daughter, but refuses to see you, all isn't lost. Children grow up. They learn. Sometimes they change their minds."

Despite his praise and reassurance, Margo felt chilled to the bone. If Sooz is mine, maybe someday she'll seek me out, she thought. Not Seth. I've lost him for good.

"Maybe." She shrugged. "I don't deserve much credit. Practically speaking, I didn't have any other choice."

Several minutes later Seth accompanied Jake back into the room. Though he didn't show it, he was deeply shaken. Margo's willingness to see his side of things had caught him by surprise. Touched, and aching at the sorrow that stared back at him from her big, dark eyes, he'd found himself agreeing to accept her proposal.

If Sooz isn't my biological daughter, I don't want to know about it, he thought fiercely. Yet with the superstructure of his anger collapsing, doubt had begun to creep in. So had memories of how he'd felt about Margo once. The memories hurt. Maybe once the tests were completed, they could get on with their lives—put the whole mess behind them. Given her promise, at least he wouldn't have to worry about custody. Or visitation. Now that he'd told Sooz the reason for their breakup, the girl wanted nothing to do with her.

He watched Margo from beneath lowered lashes as Jake spelled out the terms of their acceptance, which were basically in accord with her offer. She looked pale and cold, as if she were freezing to death. Though he told himself not to be a fool, his heart went out to her. If only she hadn't deceived him that way.

They rode down in separate elevators, a minute or two apart. Emerging from Columbia Center's imposing lobby, Seth glimpsed Margo as she mingled with a crowd of pedestrians. Except for the set of her shoulders, she looked much as she had the afternoon they'd met in the finishing shed at Danner Yachts, Inc. Her movements were brisk and graceful, her bright yellow coat a stab of color against the dreary weather.

Two weeks later Seth was at the boatworks, overseeing repairs to a yacht he'd built, when one of his mechanics handed him the portable phone. Jake Nauman was on the line.

Holding the receiver to his ear, he waved to his assistant at the helm to cut the yacht's engines. "Okay," he said, tensing up despite an earlier vow that he'd take things in his stride. "Let's have the results."

As usual, Jake didn't mince words. "It's bad news, I'm afraid," he said. "Both the blood test and the tissue evaluation that followed it were positive. Genetically speaking, there's a better than ninety-five percent chance that Margo Rourke is Susan's natural mother."

If Sooz was Margo's child, she couldn't be his. Seth felt as if he'd been kicked in the stomach. Helplessly he cursed medical science for mocking a father-daughter bond that had encompassed first steps, bedtime stories and countless jam-smeared kisses.

"Seth?" Jake asked, concern resonating in his voice. "Are you still there?"

"Yeah, I'm here." He was grasping at straws. But he had to ask. "Any chance *my* cell proteins matched Sooz's, too?"

The attorney sighed. "Sorry. But they were way off the mark. I know it's hard, but try to look at the positive side in this. Thanks to our written and notarized agreement with Mrs. Rourke, nothing has to change."

Getting a similar if more exuberant message from Tom McMillan on her answering machine when she returned home from delivering some work to a client, Margo

didn't feel much like celebrating. Granted, the relief of
finally knowing the truth had begun to seep into blood
and bone. Yet she couldn't seem to think of anything but
Seth.

All too well, she could imagine what a blow the news
would be to him. God knew she'd found it traumatic
when researchers had contacted her after Beth Ann's
death. The urge to say or do something that would ease
Seth's pain was overwhelming. Acting on impulse, she sat
down at her computer. Words flowed onto the screen.

In her letter to Seth, Margo apologized again for deceiving him.

Seth,
When I first contacted you, I didn't know what kind
of man you were. I wanted to make sure the child
who might be mine was well cared for. And loved.
Then I met you, and her. And began to love you
both. I was trapped, by my feelings for you and my
yearning to share your lives. I never meant to hurt
either of you.

I know that's no excuse. It just happens to be the
truth. I urge you not to discuss the test results with
Sooz until you're comfortable with them yourself
and you can focus on her feelings. Once you've told
her and she's had time to think about them, I hope
you'll ask her if she's willing to see me. If she isn't,
there's no need for her to visit a psychiatrist unless
you think it's advisable. I'm willing to drop the
matter, at least for the next couple of years.

Margo

Closeting himself in his home office to read what
Margo had written, Seth was astounded by her selfless-

ness. She'd been right about Sooz's genetic heritage.
Maybe she was telling the truth when she said how much
she cared for him. I'm not sure I'd be so generous if our
situations were reversed, he acknowledged, his anger
collapsing still further. Without Sooz, she has no one.
And I, for one, would find that difficult.

A shaft of regret pierced him when he thought of the
life he and Margo might have had together. The diamond she'd returned to him was still in his desk. Though
he'd lectured himself several times about returning it to
the jewelers, he'd never gotten around to doing the actual deed. Something had stayed his hand.

Unfortunately, a lot had happened since the afternoon he'd purchased it. At this point, retrieving what
they'd lost seemed an impossibility. For one thing, the
humiliation of being forced to call off their wedding at
the last minute and the problems she'd caused him with
the media were too fresh in his mind.

There were other factors, too. If he and Margo recon-
ciled, he suspected, the press would have a field day. It
would be tantamount to admitting Sooz was the child in
the baby-swap case. Meanwhile, the girl in question
wanted nothing to do with Margo. Whenever her name
came up, she characterized Margo as a "bad person."

Sadly he put the letter away. Yet as the days passed, it
continued to haunt him. Like Margo before him, he realized he'd failed to consider the opposite side of the
equation. The yearning she'd expressed to be close to the
daughter she'd lost at birth, had made him think of his
own biological child.

Not once since Margo had first broached her incredible tale of switched infants had he asked about her. He'd
never even studied her likeness, though he'd seen several

photographs of her at Margo's house, as well as the one she'd kept in her sitting room. Suddenly aware at a feeling level that his child had lived and died without him, he began to obsess on the subject of Beth Ann Rourke, who'd survived to the ripe old age of seven before taking her place among the angels.

Had she looked like him? Or Cheryl? Had she been sweet and gentle, or a little gremlin like his beloved Sooz? One Friday evening, after driving Sooz to a slumber party at her friend Jill's house, Seth couldn't restrain himself any longer. Drawn as if by a powerful magnet, he found himself on Margo's doorstep.

Her knees almost buckled when she answered the bell. Unless her imagination was playing tricks on her, *Seth* was standing there. In his parka, heavy sweater and old jeans, he looked more than a little unsure of himself.

"Won't you...come in?" she stammered, opening the door wider.

After the way he'd treated her, he'd half expected her to slam it in his face. His voice was low and a little rough. "Thanks, I will for a minute if you don't mind."

Her mind reeling with questions, she showed him into the living room. Had Sooz agreed to see her? Or, please God, was it that he still cared for her?

Seth sat somewhat awkwardly on the sofa where they'd come so close to making love. He hadn't removed his parka and, as a result, he looked about as relaxed as a wanted man at a police convention. Though the legal issues between them had been resolved, it seemed their estrangement was still in effect.

"How's Sooz?" Margo said, attempting to break the ice as she tucked her feet beneath her in an easy chair.

"Doing okay. Mrs. Johnson comes over Tuesdays and Thursdays. I found a college student to clean house three days a week."

She couldn't help but feel sad about the ease with which she'd been replaced. Afraid to ask, she forced herself to broach a subject that had made for some sleepless nights.

"I don't suppose she wants to see me."

Sighing, Seth shook his head. A small silence ensued. In it, Margo tried to remember Tom McMillan's comforting words about children changing their minds. But they didn't take the sting out of Sooz's rejection.

"Then why are you here?" she asked.

Gold-flecked hazel eyes met hers. They were filled with pain. "I've been something of an idiot," he confessed. "I never even asked . . . about the child you raised. Since it stands to reason she was my daughter . . ."

He choked up, unable to get out another word.

It took all the self-discipline she possessed not to take him in her arms. Reminding herself she didn't have the right, she got up and took a leather-bound album down from one of the bookcases.

"I have quite a few pictures of her," she offered. "Would you like to see some of them?"

He nodded, not trusting himself to speak.

"Mind if I sit by you?"

"No . . . of course not."

Unsnapping his parka and tossing it over the back of the couch, he slid over to make room for her. Moments later they were side by side, engrossed in the events of Beth Ann Rourke's life and the many photographs that had documented them.

The girl's newborn pictures didn't tell Seth much. "I guess all babies look alike," he commented with a twinge of disappointment, studying a close-up Jim had taken.

Margo recalled several baby pictures she'd seen of Sooz, in particular, one Seth kept on the dresser near his bed. She'd spent several minutes studying it the first time she'd changed his sheets.

"I wouldn't say that," she disagreed. "But you're right, in a sense. As infants, Beth and Sooz must have resembled each other quite a bit. They were about the same weight, for one thing. And they both had dark hair. I can almost see how the mixup occurred."

On the next page of the album was an enlarged, professional-looking photo of Margo nursing Beth. Seated in a bentwood rocker with her blouse unbuttoned and sunlight streaming into the room, she'd cuddled the child she'd believed was hers with a look of absolute love and devotion on her face.

Focusing on her expression, the generous swell of her engorged breast and his daughter's hungry mouth, Seth almost lost it again. His baby had landed in paradise whereas, with Cheryl, Sooz had never received much lap time. A tireless socialite who hadn't wanted to be pregnant in the first place, his ex-wife had relied heavily on pacifiers and baby-sitters.

"Who took this?" he managed at last.

"My husband."

"He was a damn good photographer."

Margo nodded, keenly aware something precious hung in the balance between them. "He did pretty well, considering how sick he was."

More pictures followed, including poses of Beth in the buff on a shaggy white rug, Beth with gobs of baby cereal on her chin learning to eat from a spoon. Turning a page, Seth suddenly found himself skipping to amateurish, overexposed shots of a sturdy eighteen-month-old, beating delightedly on a toy drum in her striped pajamas and waltzing Raggedy Andy around Margo's living room.

"What happened?" he asked. "These photos look different, as if they were taken by someone else. And there's a gap. You didn't record her first birthday."

"Jim's death happened."

Dummy, Seth taxed himself.

It was Margo's turn to endure a bittersweet moment. But it didn't last. Though she'd deeply mourned Jim's loss, it had taken place years earlier. She was over it now—as much as anyone got over such things. These days her heart was filled with longing for the living, breathing man whose muscular, denim-clad thigh was currently just inches from hers.

In Seth's opinion, the daughter he'd never known favored Cheryl most. But she'd drawn from his heritage, too. Abruptly, in a snapshot of the girl clutching a pair of Easter bunnies, he recognized his mother's smile. There was something of the late Margaret Mary Danner about her eyes, as well. Though they hadn't met in life, Beth and her paternal grandmother were together now. He brushed away a tear.

Pictures of Beth clowning around in her various Halloween costumes brought smiles, as did shots of her splashing in a backyard kiddie pool. Margo had many happy memories to relate. Yet even as she did, she braced herself. The last photo in the album, one of Beth in a brand new Brownie scout uniform, had been taken just hours before the school bus accident that had claimed her life.

When they reached that page, she couldn't help it; the tears started to flow. Not stopping to weigh the consequences, Seth slipped an arm about her shoulders. "Margo, I'm so sorry," he said.

To feel his warmth, his protectiveness surrounding her even for a moment was more than she'd hoped to experience again. "Beth was so young," she grieved, struggling for control. "When I kissed her goodbye that morning, I never dreamed it would be for the last time. Sometimes I think the place in my life where she belongs will never heal."

Yet she'd opened her heart to Sooz.

His hold on her tightened possessively. How had she managed to survive the tragedy of Beth Ann's death alone? If he'd lost Sooz under similar circumstances, he was convinced he'd have become a stark, raving maniac.

"I wish to God you'd told me about Beth and the tests up front," he said. "Maybe we could have avoided some additional heartbreak. Maybe..."

Margo guessed the words he couldn't bring himself to say would have been about the life they'd promised to share. "Would you have listened?" she queried softly. "And believed me? Or would you have been just as incredulous and upset?"

Though he didn't do so aloud, Seth had to admit she was right. He'd have been furious, though without the added twist of feeling betrayed by someone he loved. If Margo had done as she probably wished she had a thousand times over, they'd never have known or learned to care for each other.

"I miss you," he said, his confession coming straight from the heart.

It was as if a dam burst inside her. "Oh, Seth. I miss you, too."

Seconds later the barriers were down and she was in his arms. He was holding her so tightly she thought her bones would break. Though they tried, they couldn't seem to get close enough. At last he drew back a little and tilted her chin with one finger so that it was on a level with his.

"Let me stay," he begged. "Sooz is sleeping over at a friend's. I promise nothing will happen. I just need to be with you."

He hadn't said anything about loving her. Or trying to piece their shattered plans back together. Probably with Sooz feeling the way she did, he viewed marriage as an impossibility for them.

If that was true, it was risky letting him get close to her again. She was bound to be hurt by it. On the other side of the balance sheet was her love for him and the fact that, in a way most people never did, they'd shared two children. Ultimately she couldn't deny him what she wanted so much herself.

"Okay," she agreed. "But I haven't been sleeping well lately. I'm not sure I could deal with another night on the couch."

She was inviting him to share her bed.

So grateful he felt humble, Seth pulled her to her feet. They went, arm-in-arm, to the bedroom he'd never seen. Turning back an heirloom quilt and the bed's top sheet, Margo got out one of her flannel nightgowns and went into the bathroom to change.

When she came out, Seth was already under the covers, his tall frame taking up most of the available space. Pausing to turn off the lamp, she got in beside him. His mouth sought hers and, for a hot moment, the union they'd denied themselves so long seemed inevitable.

Seth wished he could justify going ahead. But he couldn't. He'd made Margo a promise and he intended to keep it. Instead of taking advantage of her, he'd put his energy into finding some kind of answer for them. Kissing her again, this time with great tenderness, he drew her head down against his shoulder.

Chapter Ten

Seth awoke to hear the shower running. By the filtered, grayish light of another rainy Seattle morning, Margo apparently had decided the better part of valor was retreat. Well, he wouldn't push his luck. First he had to undo some of the damage he'd done with Sooz.

Throwing off the covers, he zipped up his jeans over the boxer shorts he'd slept in and padded to the kitchen to make them some coffee. Much as he wanted to, he couldn't remain at the bungalow for long. In an hour, he'd have to hotfoot it back to Magnolia and pick up his daughter.

Sooz is my daughter, he reiterated, testing a time-honored formula. But so was Beth. Funny how the word's meaning had expanded for him since Margo had led him through her collection of photographs the night before. For the life of him, he wasn't sure which dark-haired moppet was actually *his,* just that he mourned not knowing the one and loved the other more than life itself.

If I'd learned about the switch before Beth died, while I still had a chance to meet her, you can bet I'd have taken it, he admitted, filling Margo's coffeepot with water and pouring it through the grid on the top of her electric drip machine. His strong feelings about Beth had finally explained Margo's motives to him in a way that he could understand.

As a small apology for not getting the message before, he decided to try his hand at scrambled eggs. They were bubbling in the pan when Margo walked into the kitchen, wearing a white terry-cloth robe that tied simply at her waist. Her hair was a mass of damp ringlets.

"Oh, babe..." he said helplessly, desire curling to life inside him.

Passion took precedence as the eggs burned. When Seth drew her into his arms, she nestled closer. He wasn't wearing a shirt and, unable to resist, he unfastened her belt, causing the front of her robe to fall open. Though her arms and back were still covered, she was completely naked against him.

For Seth, the feeling of closeness was incredible. Her nipples had hardened into tight nuggets of longing against his chest. Reaching inside the robe, he ran his hands down the fluid curves of her back to grasp her buttocks. God, but she was exquisite! Her heated flesh was as smooth as alabaster. He wanted to make love to her right there, on the kitchen floor, with an encore on the countertop.

It wasn't any secret that she wanted it, too. Never since their first kiss, also consummated in a kitchen, had her body lied to him. To think he'd claimed her attraction to him was just a scam to get at Sooz! He should have known better from the start.

With Seth's hands on her body and his tongue deep in her mouth, Margo could feel her scruples weakening. His arousal was big and hard, pressing against her thigh. She wanted him inside her. What did it matter if she couldn't keep him for a lifetime? She wasn't proud where he was concerned. She'd take whatever she could get.

Once again it was Seth who stopped them. "I haven't earned the right to do this yet," he explained, drawing the front of her robe together. "First, I have a few things to work out. I know a lot has happened in the past couple of months that seems insurmountable. But there's got to be a way for us. Somehow, I'm going to find it."

Margo wanted to believe him so much that there was a hollow place inside her. But she wasn't sure he could. Sooz had her back up, and she was no pushover. After Seth left, kissing her goodbye at the door, she put the skillet, scorched eggs and all, into the sink to soak and phoned Nell.

"Seth spent the night with me," she confided, secure in the knowledge that her longtime friend could keep a secret.

Nell whistled. "You're kidding!"

"Nothing happened. That is, we didn't make love. But we slept in the same bed. Apparently it hit him at gut level that, if I gave birth to Sooz, then Beth Ann must have been his child. He came over looking pretty desperate and I offered to show him some pictures. One thing led to another, and we ended up in each other's arms."

Her friend was clearly delighted. "But that's wonderful, hon!" she exclaimed. "I know how much the breakup hurt you. By the way, where was Sooz while all this was going on?''

"Staying over with a friend. Nell...I think Seth wants us to get back together. But I'm not sure he can pull it off, given Sooz's renewed antipathy to me. What do the stars suggest?''

True to form, Nell had already checked them out. "Not much," she said. "Just that there's a break-through in your chart, indicating new possibilities.''

Margo didn't have any problem with that. "What about Sooz?" she persisted. "Any chance she might be willing to let bygones be bygones?''

On that point, it seemed, both her stars and the girl's were mute. "Maybe I'm going out on a limb by saying this," Nell admitted, "but what I originally told you when I drew up her chart still applies. Sooz is a Sagittarius. And, though Sags never forget, they *do* forgive. I have a feeling that, deep down, she misses you. And cares about you very much.''

Broaching the subject of a possible détente with Margo to the prickly, outspoken little girl in question, Seth hit a brick wall.

"Margo Rourke is a bad person," she declared in no uncertain terms. "She lied to us and made up a story so she could take me away from you. I don't ever want to see her again.''

While he'd been fighting Margo's lawsuit and his own inner battles, it seemed, Sooz had been constructing an emotional fortress.

"That's not quite true, pumpkin," he countered, inviting her onto his lap. "I should have explained before, but her story about you and another baby being switched wasn't phony after all. It really happened. Remember the finger stick that was part of your checkup at the doctor's office? Well, some blood and a few tissue cells from that stick got tested, and they proved Margo right. Before you and her daughter were born, you were in her tummy, and her daughter was in your mom's. You got switched accidentally at the hospital.''

A look of sheer panic came over Sooz's face. "No, Daddy! No! Please don't say that!"

Soothingly, he kissed her forehead. "Why not? It's true, sweetheart."

Tears welled in Sooz's eyes. "Does that mean . . . you don't want to be my daddy anymore?"

"Of course it doesn't!" The hug he gave her was fierce. "You'll never have to worry about that."

"I will if Margo comes back," she predicted darkly, burying her face against his shoulder.

Distraught, Seth didn't contact Margo for several days. Or tackle Sooz on the subject of a reconciliation again. He didn't want to hold out false hope, or upset his child needlessly. Yet without the woman he'd learned to love so profoundly, life was a basic shade of gray. In his opinion, doing without her might even be injurious to his health. Though he was almost never sick, he'd caught a cold, damn it. He couldn't sleep, or seem to concentrate at work.

After a great deal of soul-searching, he decided that, while parents owed their children love and the best possible upbringing, they weren't obliged unnecessarily to throw away their own happiness. Sooz was just nine years old. His divorce from Cheryl and aborted wedding with Margo, followed by the discovery that she'd been unintentionally switched with another infant at birth, had been extremely upsetting for Sooz. But with time and lots of affection, he believed, she'd adjust.

The sixth sense he'd developed as a single father told him that, in her heart, Sooz *wanted* him to set things right. After the way she'd handled the girl during her tenure as their housekeeper, there wasn't any doubt in his mind that Margo would be good for her. God knew she could use some of the luminous, selfless devotion that had flooded the photograph of Margo nursing Beth.

The conclusion he drew propelled him back to Margo's door. To his chagrin, she didn't seem to be at home, though her car was parked in the drive. Had something happened to her? Restlessly pacing back and forth on her front sidewalk, he began to arouse a certain degree of curiosity among the neighbors.

At last Margo appeared, struggling out of a taxi with several bags of groceries in her arms.

"Where have you been?" he demanded. "I've been worried about you. With the M.G. in the drive..."

Abruptly aware of how burdened down she was, he took the groceries from her and stood there waiting for an explanation.

"Sorry I didn't notify you my car was on the fritz," she replied tartly, unable to hide her amusement and relief at seeing him. "I didn't realize you'd volunteered to be my keeper."

"For your information, I have a strong interest in everything that concerns you," he answered. "I want you to be my wife, if you'll have me after everything we've been through. To be perfectly honest, I've never stopped wanting it...not even when I was at my most furious. Say you'll give me another chance."

They were still squared off on the sidewalk and Margo was suddenly afraid to move or take a breath. "What about Sooz?'' she asked faintly. "I can't believe she'd approve. Or allow herself to trust me again."

At the mention of his favorite prickly pear, Seth shook his head in frustration. "Sooz is being opinionated and contrary, as usual," he confessed. "In my judgment, it's her way of fighting the fear that she'll lose me now that we've learned she isn't my natural daughter. I can't prove it. But I think that, beneath all her hostility, she still cares for you. I know for a fact she was much happier when the three of us were together."

It was uncanny the way his words echoed Nell's. "Do you honestly think so?" Margo said hopefully.

"Yes," Seth told her. "Most definitely *yes.*"

Since coming to a decision, he'd had a one-track mind. It wasn't focused on practical things. Setting the grocery bags down in a puddle without giving a moment's thought to the fact that they might disintegrate, he took her in his arms. "If you're willing to trust me on this," he added lovingly, "don't you think it's time you answered *yes?* And that we sealed the bargain with a kiss?"

They were married a week later at the King County Courthouse, without Sooz's blessing, though Seth had insisted she be present. Held in the chambers of a judge who had known his parents, the brief ceremony was unlike the one they'd originally planned in almost every respect. The only exception was that Nell and Seth's brother Bob stood up for them. Because of Sooz's opposition, they hadn't asked her to take part.

Joy Danner, Seth's sister-in-law, held Sooz by the hand. Staring down at her shoes, the girl looked as if she wanted to make a break for it. When everyone had met downstairs, by the courthouse lobby's information desk, she'd refused even to speak to Margo. The immediate future looked bleak from the standpoint of establishing a mother-daughter relationship.

Nervous and not totally convinced that they were doing the right thing, Margo wore a plain navy suit and white silk blouse with a white orchid on her lapel. As she and Seth spoke their vows, she could feel Sooz's resentment enfolding her like a cloud.

It was difficult for her to believe the wedding was actually taking place. After giving up hope of ever seeing Seth again, she would be his wife, and her own daughter's stepmother. If only past traumas could be erased and they could start afresh, with full knowledge of their fatefully interconnected relationships, from the moment he and Sooz had tickled her as she lay in bed.

Both her wedding ring and the diamond she'd returned to Seth were on her finger as he drew her into his arms for a nuptial kiss. Suddenly, miraculously, everything felt right. With his mouth on hers and his hard, tall body pressed against her, she knew with the deepest kind of knowing that here was a man she'd always been destined to meet and love—one who, over the course of many lifetimes, if Nell's astrological and karmic beliefs were correct, had helped to integrate and complete her evolving self.

They weren't separated by any more secrets. He'd forgiven her for her deception and she'd let go of her prodigious hurt. Whatever their problems with Sooz, Seth would make her feel protected and cherished. She wouldn't have to face the girl's resentment alone.

Abandoning her need to take full responsibility for everyone's well-being and their capacity to recover from what had been a very difficult situation, she let herself merge with him. Hadn't he insisted they had a right to be happy? And promised her everything would be all right?

Her spurt of confidence faltered a few minutes later as they entered the elegant lobby of the Westin Hotel, with its mirrored ceiling, broad gold pillars and cocoa patterned carpet. Sooz wouldn't look at her *or* Seth. Her footsteps dragged as he ushered them into the gardenlike Palm Court Restaurant for their wedding lunch.

Seated directly across from Sooz at the round, peach-linen-napped table they'd reserved beneath the Palm Court's soaring glass-roofed gazebo and crystal chandelier, the girl barely spoke when spoken to, even by her uncle and aunt. She spent most of the meal toying with the food on her plate.

Likewise, though they were painstakingly polite and made lame attempts at jocularity, neither Bob nor Joy Danner seemed to be enjoying themselves very much. It was obvious they couldn't forget Seth's aborted January 15th wedding and its painful aftermath. That afternoon he'd informed their assembled guests, somewhat cryptically, that an impediment to their marriage had come up. And it was clear to Margo that her new in-laws still considered the tangled relationships caused by the inadvertent swap of their infant niece a strong barrier. She got the strong impression they thought Joy's cousin would have been a far more suitable mate for Seth.

At last it was time for them to leave on their honeymoon. Bob and Joy offered to drive Sooz home, where she'd be looked after by Mrs. Johnson until her parents returned at the end of the week. Hoping to distance herself from their earlier fiasco, Margo had insisted she didn't want a San Francisco wedding trip. She'd succeeded in convincing Seth she'd much prefer spending what time they had alone with him at his San Juan Island hideaway.

Beaming, Nell congratulated Seth. She hugged Margo as he went to fetch the car. "Relax, hon," she suggested. "Sagittarians like Sooz aren't won over in a day. It might take a while. On the bright side, you've got a fabulous new husband you happen to be crazy about. And, according to the stars, the worst is over. Of course, there might be a few minor glitches yet."

"Related to Sooz, no doubt," Margo predicted.

Her friend responded with a helpless shrug. "To tell you the truth, her chart isn't totally auspicious for the next few days. But after that, it's clear sailing."

Margo groaned. "The next few days just happen to coincide with our honeymoon! If I thought anything bad would happen to her..."

"Spoken like a true mom." Nell patted her shoulder reassuringly. "As I've told you before, the planets only incline. *We* translate inclination into reality. The feeling I get from studying Sooz's astrological influences is that she needs to learn a lesson here. And that you should go off on your honeymoon and let her learn it. If it'll make you feel any better, I'll look in on her and Mrs. Johnson..."

"*Would* you?" Margo was overcome with relief. "Oh, Nell... I'd really appreciate it!"

Just then, Seth drove up in the Mercedes. Putting it in park, he got out and came around to install his bride in the passenger seat.

"Bon voyage!" Nell called out, digging a surprise handful of rice out of her pocket and tossing it at them. "Have a wonderful time! Everything's going to be okay."

Locking up the Mercedes in the fenced storage area outside the boatworks, they changed into casual clothes in Seth's office and boarded his yacht. Everything was ready to go. To make sure of that, he'd stowed their luggage away, along with all the provisions they could possibly need, the previous afternoon.

Kissing her lingeringly and with love, he gave the order to cast off. With Margo performing the duties of first mate, they edged out into Lake Union, heading west toward the Lake Washington ship canal and Puget Sound.

It was a soft, silver-gray Seattle afternoon, with rain clouds dissipating and a moonstone glimmer of sunlight peeking through. The temperature was in the upper fifties. Though it was brisk on the water, they were dressed for it in waterproof parkas, jeans, sweaters and flannel shirts.

"Going up to San Juan was a great idea," Seth affirmed, tugging Margo close to him when she joined him on the yacht's flying bridge. "You...me...alone together. With no telephones and no responsibilities. Maybe we won't stop there. What do you say we head on up to Alaska? We could build our own igloo and make love for a month."

After so much unhappiness and frustrated desire, running away together for an extended period was lovely to dream about. But they both knew it was an impossibility. With Sooz in her current troubled state, a few days was the most they could snatch.

Having Seth would be enough for her. "It sounds like heaven," she answered, standing on tiptoe to nuzzle a warm kiss against his neck.

It was a slow day at the locks and they passed through with record speed. Wind whipped at their hair as they entered the Sound and turned north toward Admiralty Inlet and their destination. Seth pushed the throttles to three-quarters full. At that speed, he estimated, the trip to San Juan would take them five hours.

They reached his cottage near Turn Point at sunset. As they tied up at the floating dock and unloaded the essentials, lights winked on in some of the other dwellings scattered along the shore. The water was silver-blue with a delicate sheen of peach. Backlit by the waning glow in the west, a few clouds that had turned the deep purple-blue of iris floated overhead.

As she and Seth started up the dock's cantilevered steps, Margo's excitement grew. In a matter of minutes now, their provisions would be put away in the cottage's refrigerator. Seth would build a fire in the two-way hearth that separated its living area from the master bedroom. They'd disrobe by its flickering radiance, making love to each other first with their eyes.

Seth had been thinking similar thoughts all afternoon. Like Margo, he'd imagined a slow, exquisite seduction. Before entering her and driving them to their first consummation, he'd wanted to make her crazy with wanting him.

Now sheer lust to claim her was uppermost. As they gained the top of the wooden staircase that scaled the bluff and stood on the cottage's rustic deck while he fitted his key into the lock, he paused and turned to her.

"I hope you're not hungry," he announced, his voice harsh with barely suppressed emotion. "Because all I want is you."

They were entwined before they were halfway through the door—tugging at parka snaps and mauling each other with deep, intrusive kisses as they closed it. Exercising the right she'd given him that afternoon, Seth helped pull her sweater over her head. Her eyes darkening to pools of velvet, she reciprocated. With unceremonious haste, buttons were separated from their buttonholes.

In the picnic cooler at their feet, the perishables could wait. So could the fire, though the redwood-and-stone cottage was breathtakingly cold. Naked to the waist, they rubbed against each other, her nipples puckering against his reddish-gold mat of chest hair, his hips thrusting forward so that he could caress her with the bulk of his desire.

In response, a fire pit of longing opened between her legs. At the very core of her being, she was desperate to contain him. "Oh, Seth," she cried, the words barely above a whisper. "Please ... take me to bed."

Chapter Eleven

There'd be no scruples, no barrier of clothing to separate them. With a groan, Seth lifted her off her feet. Her fingers meshed in his thick, red hair, she wrapped her legs around him. He was all man, solid as a tree trunk in her arms, and miraculously hers.

"God, but I love you!" he confessed, kissing her mouth, her nose, her eyelids with passionate urgency.

"Seth, darling... I love you, too."

Already she was part of him. Before they'd ever met, she'd nursed his baby. And he'd raised hers. Now they could make one together.

"Don't let's use anything," she pleaded, seized by an uncontrollable impulse as he carried her into the shadowed, unfamiliar room where they'd consummate their vows. "Now that you're mine, I want to risk it all."

Spontaneous though they were, the words echoed her dearest wishes. It's what I've wanted from the beginning, she realized, though the urge wasn't conscious until this moment.

Seth was stunned. His first wife had never said anything like that to him. Now the petite, dark-haired Gypsy he ached to possess would let him come flooding into her. She'd welcome the presence of his seed in her body without protection. The utter commitment and deep surrender that entailed caused him to lose the scattered remnants of his self-control.

Lowering her to the brass-framed bed, which was spread with a down comforter, he unzipped her jeans and dragged them down her legs. The lacy triangle of her bikini panties followed, to be tossed on the floor beside her shoes and socks.

Dropping to his knees, he lavished kisses on her upturned breasts, the yielding vulnerability of her stomach. Her skin was like cream, or velvet.

"Did you really mean it?" he asked, raising his head from the coarse nest of curls that guarded her feminine portal.

Her eyes glittered with love for him in the dark. "I've been empty of you all my life," she whispered, her hands claiming the broad, sweet shape of his shoulders. "I don't know what would make me happier."

Neither did he, though he hadn't been planning anything of the sort. Why *not* now? he thought, the idea taking hold of him. We're both in our thirties. There's no reason to wait.

Fired by the almost mystical connection they'd forge, he parted her velvet folds. She was liquid with wanting him. Hungrily he searched out the nub of her desire, to tease it gently, then more emphatically with a rhythmic, circular motion. Darting deeper, his tongue returned to its loving task.

Margo writhed in ecstasy at the helpless blossoming of her desire. Like the petals of an exotic flower opening in time-lapse photography, its ripples unfolded, each over-lapping the next with greater and greater fervency. With every breath she took, release moved closer within her grasp.

I want it to happen with him inside me, she thought frantically. With us fused together like one person.

"Oh, please..."

Seth was burning up with need. "Tell me what to do," he pleaded in a passion-drugged voice. "Do you want it this way? Or..."

Her hair was a tangle of curls against the puffy, chan-nel-quilted coverlet. "I want...you and me...rocketing off together."

He didn't need a second invitation. Taking off his shoes and unzipping his jeans, he kicked them aside. Though the room was still icy cold, neither of them felt it. From her prone position, Margo ravished him with her eyes.

Lying there with her arms outstretched and her thighs spread apart like wings, she looked like heaven to him. Would the difference in their heights, his added weight, be a burden to her? He'd try not to crush her too much.

She wouldn't let him ride low, or rest the lion's share of his weight on his elbows. Instead, as they fitted them-selves together, she shifted position so that her face was half buried against the hairy mat of his chest and she bore the full brunt of him.

"Sweetheart, you'll smother..." Seth protested, his hand between their bodies, coaxing her back to the heights.

"No, I won't." She moaned with pleasure, lifting her hips from the bed. "I want...you this way. I can *feel* you best."

Incredibly she was right. When they began to move, with Margo thrusting her lower body into him and Seth grazing the apex of her sensitivity on each downward stroke, the contact they made was electric. Each time he withdrew and entered, he seemed to go deeper. Her strong inner muscles grasped and released him in erotic point counterpoint.

Their profound need for each other and the unbearably exquisite pressure they were exerting wouldn't let them last. Though Seth tried to maintain their rhythm or even slow it, the radiance of their arousal seemed to grow until it was a halo surrounding them.

Suddenly they broke free, reaching their peak just seconds apart. As he filled her the way she'd begged him to, the tidal wave of sensation that engulfed them was almost global. Together his archangel brightness and her dark, feminine mysteries shook the universe.

They made love twice more before curling to sleep beneath the down comforter as, in the woods outside the cottage, a soft rain began to fall.

The following morning, the sun was out. Pleasuring each other again, showering and starting for the kitchen, they decided they wanted more and spent an additional half hour in bed. At last the craving of their empty stomachs for food drove them to make coffee and an omelet.

"You know, a honeymoon isn't supposed to be *all* sex." Seth grinned, utterly sated and content with his existence as he polished off a man-size portion of eggs with the appetite of a lumberjack. "What do you say we go into town...bum around a little after stopping by Harve Bjorn's place to see if there've been any calls?''

Harve Bjorn was an old friend of Seth's who owned and operated an art gallery in Friday Harbor. Since the Danner cottage didn't have a phone, when they'd decided on a San Juan honeymoon, Seth had called him to ask if they might leave the gallery number with Mrs. Johnson in case a problem arose.

Pausing with her coffee cup halfway to her mouth, Margo remembered Nell's reluctant admission that Sooz's horoscope wasn't ''totally auspicious for the next few days.''

''Do you think everything's all right?'' she asked worriedly, a breath of apprehension ruffling the hairs on the back of her neck.

As close as they'd become during the past twenty-four hours, Seth didn't share her concern. ''What could happen?'' he replied. ''It's probably safe to say Sooz is still steaming. A few days to cool down and think things over will be good for her. Besides, Mrs. Johnson's eminently reliable. Aren't you curious how we're going to get from here to civilization?''

They'd come by boat. ''The yacht, I suppose,'' Margo answered, temporarily distracted from her fears. ''Or should I put on my hiking boots?''

Seth's grin widened. ''I have to admit they'd look pretty cute with my favorite white robe and what's underneath it. But they won't be necessary. Your tennies will do.''

His mood reassured her. Dimpling, she tilted her head to one side. ''What shall I wear?''

''How about your best black leather jacket? Bob and I keep a motorcycle in the shed.''

The cottage was situated off a winding gravel thoroughfare known as Pear Point Road. Seated on the back of Seth's motorcycle, with her arms wound tightly around him, the breeze disarranging her hair and sunlight glancing through the trees, Margo felt as if she didn't have a care in the world. With Seth as her husband, she could handle whatever fate had in store.

Rising steeply from its ferry dock, Friday Harbor was a charming collection of little restaurants, gift shops, bookstores and everyday emporialike hardware stores and supermarkets. There was even a movie theater.

Harve Bjorn's gallery was on Spring Street. Deciding that she'd been crazy to borrow trouble, Margo was looking forward to enjoying its surprisingly fine collection of paintings when Harve himself greeted them with a relieved expression.

"Thank heaven you're here," he said. "I was about to close up shop and drive out to your place. Someone just called and left an urgent message. You're to phone home right away."

"Oh, no..." Margo rested one hand on Seth's arm for support.

He shook his head. "It's probably nothing." Yet, as he dialed his Magnolia number, a concerned frown drew his blond brows together.

Nell answered on the first ring. The gallery had a speaker phone, and Margo was able to listen in on the conversation.

"I'm sorry to have to tell you this," her friend said over audible expressions of distress from Mrs. Johnson in the background, "but Sooz has disappeared."

She'd run away. Margo's heart sank. This is all my fault, she thought.

Seth's expression was a blend of outrage and fear for their daughter's safety as he ground out a question.

"When did this happen?"

"Just this morning." There wasn't much doubt Nell, too, was upset. Yet she seemed to be keeping a cool head.

"Sooz didn't turn up at school," she elaborated. "Apparently her friend, Jill Lancaster, knew about it, got scared and told. The principal phoned Mrs. Johnson about ten o'clock."

Seth was looking more disturbed by the moment. "Did Jill say anything else?" he asked.

"When pressed, she mentioned something about your first wife passing through town on her way home from Hawaii. It seems she called just a few hours after you left and Sooz talked to her, though Mrs. Johnson didn't know anything about it. We think it's possible Sooz left to be with her. But we don't know where the Magnusons might be staying. Or even if they've arrived yet."

Damn Sooz, Seth thought. Doesn't she know how much we love her? Why can't she see Cheryl is *nobody's* refuge?

With a churning feeling in the pit of his stomach, he related the name of the hotel where his ex-wife and her new husband had stayed on their trip east. "Have you called the police?" he said, causing Margo to wince.

Nell had. She was keeping in close touch with them.

"I don't know how to thank you," Seth told her. "Can you hang around until we get there? We'll be back just as quickly as the *Sea Wind* can carry us."

Romance was the furthest thing from their minds as they roared back to the cottage, Seth's motorcycle trailing a cloud of gravel dust. Within minutes they were aboard the yacht, slicing full speed ahead through the frigid blue water that separated them from Seattle. Half sick with guilt for what she believed was her selfishness in accepting Seth's proposal and allowing him to take her away on a honeymoon trip when Sooz was so upset, Margo shrank further and further into herself.

They were within sight of Shilshole Bay and the mouth of the ship canal when Seth couldn't stand it any longer. It had been heartrending enough to learn Sooz was missing. He couldn't bear it if Margo withdrew from him, too.

"Look at me," he ordered with fire in his eyes, momentarily letting go of the wheel and grasping her by the shoulders. "I want you to believe it when I say none of this is your fault. We have a right to each other!"

Sooz was still missing when, with a lurch of the Mercedes' brakes, they drew up at the house. There was an unfamiliar car in the drive. The police detective assigned to look for her had returned to question Mrs. Johnson and Nell further.

"Mr. Danner," he said, pre-empting Mrs. Johnson's tearful apologies. "I'm glad you're back. The hotel you mentioned has no reservation for your ex-wife and her husband. And we've checked most of the others. Can you think of any other arrangement they might have made?"

Seth wanted to kick himself. In the upset over Sooz's disappearance, he hadn't thought of Cheryl's widowed aunt, Roberta Kuhn, who lived a short distance from them on the north side of Magnolia, near Discovery Park. That is, she did when she wasn't supervising her ranch in the eastern part of the state. On at least one occasion, Cheryl and Tom Magnuson had stayed with her there.

A bit shamefacedly, he related the information.

The detective nodded. "I think we should check with Mrs. Kuhn right away."

Though they let the phone ring at least twenty times, no one answered at the Kuhn residence. Still, it was their only lead. Leaving Nell and Mrs. Johnson in charge of the home front, Seth and Margo got back into the Mercedes to follow the detective to Roberta Kuhn's residence.

Margo had laced her fingers nervously through Seth's, forcing him to drive left-handed. "What if we don't find her?" she whispered.

His reply was fierce. "That simply isn't an option."

Like many of its neighbors situated above the ship canal west of the locks, Roberta Kuhn's modern redwood home had been built on a steep hillside with several decks supported by pilings at the rear. Nobody answered when they rang the bell.

Peering inside the front windows, the detective decided to question the neighbors. "Wait here," he instructed. "I'll be back in a moment."

Seth shook his head. "I'm going to check the back entrance."

"And *I'm* coming with you."

Slipping and sliding down the rocky descent, Margo scrambled after him. Thorns from some of the natural plantings that helped to protect the steep grade from erosion caught at her jeans, but she didn't notice. All she cared about was finding the precious but stubborn little girl she'd lost at birth and only just found again.

If Sooz won't forgive me and agree that we can live as a family, I'll bow out of the picture, she thought, fighting back the tears that threatened to obstruct her vision. Never mind how much I love Seth, or what we've come to mean to each other. We have to place our daughter's needs first. She didn't stop to think she might already be carrying another child.

Apparently the basement that opened from the concrete pad beneath Mrs. Kuhn's lower deck, was a laundry and storage area. Peering through its somewhat dusty windows, they could see an array of packing boxes and discarded tools. A washer, dryer and laundry tub were arranged side by side. There wasn't any sign of Sooz.

"Looks like we made the climb down here for nothing," Seth sighed. "The door and windows are locked. Even if she tried, Sooz couldn't possibly have gotten in this way."

Margo wasn't so sure. She'd spotted a dog entry, the kind of small, square opening with a swinging flap people sometimes used at the front of a house to facilitate newspaper delivery. It was too small for most adults to squeeze through. But a child? Or someone with Margo's petite, slender build? Either seemed a possibility.

"I know Sooz could be in a thousand different places," Margo admitted. "But something tells me this is the one. She might have crawled through that dog door. Maybe it's breaking and entering, but I'm going to investigate."

Seth grabbed her by the back of her sweater when he realized what her intentions were. "You can't, sweetheart," he protested. "It's too small. You'll get stuck."

"No. I don't think so."

Though it was a tight fit, by compressing her arms against her body, Margo managed to drag herself through the tiny opening. Getting to her feet and dusting herself off, she stood very still for a moment, just listening. She thought she'd heard a sound from one of the floors above.

Whatever the slight noise had been, it wasn't repeated. Unlocking the back door, she let Seth into the house.

Checking out the basement area and finding nothing, he started up the stairs. "Sooz," he called, "it's Daddy! If you're here, please answer me!"

The sound of a chair scraping against wooden flooring met their ears. *"Oh, Daddy..."* Sooz cried.

Seconds later she was scampering down the stairs and flinging herself into Seth's arms. Scooping her up, he held her as if he'd never let her go. Her feet dangled from grubby corduroy slacks in scuffed shoes and snagged cotton anklets as she buried her face against his neck. Margo watched from the step below them, tears of relief and sorrow for what she might be about to lose spilling though she tried not to let them.

Just then a car door slammed. After a brief hiatus, someone inserted a key into the front door lock. "What's going on?" Cheryl's voice said.

The detective was right behind her. "Mrs. Magnuson?" he asked.

They both stared as Seth gained the upper level carrying Sooz, with Margo following him.

"Mommy!" Sooz exclaimed though she continued to hold tightly to Seth. "You said you'd be here today. And you weren't. Neither was Aunt Roberta. It started to rain and I climbed down the hillside so I could get in through Tuffy's door and wait for you."

Cheryl didn't come forward to offer a hug or kiss. Instead she deposited her armload of department-store shopping bags on a nearby chair and rested expensively manicured hands on her slender hips.

"That's crazy," she said. "We might have been gone already. I *told* you we might not have time to see you this trip."

When nobody said anything in response to that, she looked at each of them in turn, her eyes narrowing slightly when they rested on Margo. "I want to know what's going *on* here," she demanded.

In a superficial way, she resembles me, Margo thought with a devastating flash of insight. But she doesn't have a heart.

Seth explained in something of a monotone. "This is my wife, Margo," he said. "And Detective Ryan, who's been helping us look for Sooz. Margo and I were married yesterday. We were on our honeymoon when we got a call that Sooz had run away. Once we learned you'd be in the area, we thought she might have run to you. Since you weren't registered at any of the better hotels..."

He'd already told Cheryl about the test results and Margo's agreement not to seek custody. But he hadn't gotten in touch with her since he and Margo had made up their differences. It was clear to him that Cheryl had no interest in the daughter she'd never known. In his opinion, his ex-wife had reacted to the truth about Sooz's parentage by distancing herself even further from the living child who loved her so much. He didn't have to add that Sooz was opposed to his remarriage. Understanding of that painful fact was written all over Cheryl's beautiful face.

She turned to the girl who, prior to Margo's revelations, she'd had no reason to think wasn't her natural daughter. "Running away was wrong," she said severely. "You must never do it again."

A tear rolled down Sooz's cheek. "I thought I could come and live with you in Hawaii, Mommy," she said in a small voice. It was apparent, though, that she'd all but reconsidered.

Obviously not stupid, Cheryl seemed to catch the girl's change of heart at once. "You know that's nonsense, Sooz," she said with a relieved smile. "This isn't even a good time for you to visit. You have school and, the minute we get home, Tom and I will be leaving for Australia and New Zealand. I want you to calm down and use a little common sense. People get remarried every day. The best place for you is here in Seattle, with your father."

"Yes, Mommy," Sooz said obediently.

With a potential crisis averted, Cheryl began to behave a little more like an affectionate parent, though her range in that department was clearly limited. She still didn't hug Sooz. But she kissed her on the cheek.

"Maybe next summer..." she murmured.

It was easy to see that, though the child Margo loved so much might wish to delude herself, she knew "next summer" would never materialize.

Margo drove the Mercedes on their way home, with Sooz sitting so close to Seth, she was practically in his lap. The girl stubbornly refused to look at her.

Nell and Mrs. Johnson were weak-kneed with relief when they walked in the door. Sending Sooz upstairs with the latter to wash and change, Seth paused to give Nell the particulars of how they'd found her.

"I want to thank you for all you've done," he added, shaking Nell's hand. "You've been a wonderful help to us. I know you've got a life apart from my family's, but I wonder if you could stick around for a few minutes...keep Margo company. I've got to get upstairs and corral you-know-who for a father-daughter talk."

Nell replied that she'd be happy to. "I'm glad I have the time," she said. "Tonight, I'm working the graveyard shift."

Surrounding Margo with a brief, hard hug that promised *later we'll talk,* Seth ran up the steps and vanished into Sooz's room. Having supervised a quick sponge bath and change into pajamas, Mrs. Johnson came down almost immediately and called a cab. After she'd gone, Margo fixed herself and Nell each a cup of tea. They sat across from each other at the kitchen table.

"Okay, hon," Nell said, giving her an inquisitive look. "Let's have it. Was it meeting Cheryl that's still upsetting you so? Or Sooz's rejection? I told you..."

"I know. That it'll take time for Sooz to get over everything's that's happened. I wish I could agree with you. But I'm not sure she will. I hate to say this because I love him so much...more than I ever dreamed it was possible to love anyone. But I think marrying Seth was a mistake."

For several minutes Nell listened quietly, allowing Margo to vent her feelings. Then, "It sounds to me like your negative Gemini twin is in the ascendant," she remarked. "Why not change over to your positive side and see if you can't weather this. Even in the middle of a crisis, a person can't look at you and Seth together and not know your marriage is right."

By now it felt to Margo as if the two of them were one person. But she didn't want to hurt him, or the child they shared. "What if Sooz can't forgive me?" she asked.

Nell reached across the table to squeeze her hand. "My reading of her horoscope yesterday still stands. There's smooth sailing ahead if you can just hang in there a little longer. I dare you to tell me she and Seth aren't worth the effort!"

It was a long, long time before Seth reappeared. By then, Nell had headed home to catch a nap before going on duty at the hospital. The sun was setting over Puget Sound. Exactly twenty-four hours had elapsed since he and Margo had tied up at the dock below his cottage with lovemaking on their minds.

He found her in the kitchen. Guessing he'd order Sooz to eat in her room, she'd prepared a dinner tray.

"I hope you're hanging in there with me, sweetheart," he said, echoing Nell's words as he put his arms around her.

"I'm doing my best," she answered. Already the survivor of too much heartbreak, she knew losing him would be more than she could take. But what if Sooz *wouldn't* relent?

When Seth took the tray upstairs, he didn't linger. A short time later, he and Margo shared wine and cheese in front of a crackling fire as he gradually filled her in on his conversation with the girl he termed "our daughter."

"For me, the turning point in the mess we made of things came when I realized at gut level that Beth was my child," he said. "I started wanting to know her, even though it was too late. This evening, some angel on my shoulder prompted me to explain that to Sooz. I emphasized that, while her biological father had died, too, you were still here, and loved her very much. I reminded her that you could tell her about Jim. She was awfully quiet after that. I think she's reconsidering."

Margo didn't dare believe it. Leaving their dishes in the sink, they went upstairs to the room where, previously, Seth had slept alone. Though she didn't expect them to make love that night, suddenly they were clinging to each other. Their adjustment as sex partners had been almost instantaneous and, though their coupling was brief, they both reached fulfillment.

Afterward Seth drew her head against his shoulder. "I love you, sweetheart," he said.

If only things were that simple, Margo thought. "I love you, too," she reciprocated, placing a kiss in the vicinity of his collarbone and adding silently, *I hope I get to keep you.*

As the rhythm of his breathing relaxed into sleep, she lay awake at his side, staring at the ceiling and wondering what lay ahead.

Chapter Twelve

When she woke, Seth was still sprawled beside her on his stomach. Always a bit unruly, his red-gold hair was wildly unkempt, as if it had been combed by a whirlwind. The straw-colored lashes she admired so much brushed the hard cheekbones of his man's face like a little boy's.

He'd turned toward her in his sleep. How I love him now, she thought. My feelings go deeper with every second. The simple act of lying here beside him under the covers is paradise.

For the second night running, they hadn't used birth control. She'd told him it would please her to have his child, and he'd taken her at her word. Apparently in his view the matter was settled. To hint that she had second thoughts now might inflict damage on their relationship that could never be reversed.

He'd never understand if she tried to explain her reservations. Yet during the past twenty-four hours she'd begun to believe a baby might exacerbate the problems they faced. When she'd told him she wanted to risk everything, she hadn't known Sooz would run away, or felt quite so pessimistic about regaining her child's friendship and trust.

Baby or no baby, the happiness she and Seth had been reaching for when they'd agreed to wed wouldn't materialize if he was forever torn between her and Sooz. Each time he backed up her authority or took her part, the girl would become more withdrawn and hostile. Ultimately Seth would lose what she'd already lost.

She didn't want that for him. Or to build a wall between him and the outspoken nine-year-old he adored. Yet a life without them didn't even bear thinking about. At the moment, the only thing she could do was to keep a cool head—try to hang in there, as Nell had said.

I hope Seth can sleep awhile, she thought, getting out of bed and putting on her robe and slippers. He's not expected at the boat yard for several days, and Sooz's disappearance was pretty rough on him.

With a lingering glance at his tawny head against the pillow, she headed downstairs to make pancake batter and squeeze fresh orange juice for their breakfast. Lining up the ingredients on the familiar island counter where she and Sooz had made so many batches of cookies and hot chocolate, she didn't see or hear Sooz come into the kitchen in her bunny-ear slippers and quilted robe, with Bear clutched tightly to her chest.

"Can I help?" the girl asked in a tentative voice.

Margo was careful to wipe the surprise off her face before she turned around. "Sure...why not?" she answered. "How would you like to break the eggs?"

Clearly pleased to be given a task that required manual dexterity, Sooz placed Bear where he could watch the proceedings and clambered up on the stool. "In the glass cup, right?" she asked. "How many do you want?"

Margo didn't have the heart to tell her to put on an apron. For several minutes, they worked quietly together, exchanging just the necessary information to carry out their task. At last the batter was made. The electric skillet ready. And the orange juice squeezed. Sooz had even set the kitchen table. There were three places, complete with place mats, napkins and silverware.

Can it be, Margo asked herself, that a *family* will sit down this morning to eat together? Though it had begun to seem like a possibility, she didn't dare hope too much.

Meanwhile, there wasn't any rush. She didn't want to wake Seth before he was ready. And, since it was a teacher's in-service training day, Sooz didn't have to hurry off to school. The day stretched before them, unmarked by conflict or harmony, a blank slate.

Not sure what her next move should be, Margo made a point of cleaning up every trace of their cooking clutter in order to give herself time to think. Initially, she knew, any balance she and Sooz struck would be a delicate one. She didn't want to make any more mistakes.

Watching her, Sooz twisted a lock of her hair. "When I talked to Daddy last night," she said slowly, "he told me you had pictures of your little girl. And the man those tests proved was…" She paused, obviously not ready yet to acknowledge a relationship that still troubled her. "I mean, the man who died, who used to be your husband," she finished instead.

Margo nodded, stunned she would broach the subject at all. "You understand, don't you," she replied after a moment, "that the mixup changed things? It made Beth mine, even though I didn't give birth to her. And it made you belong to your daddy. You always will."

Though she didn't answer Margo's question directly, Sooz seemed reassured. "I was wondering..." she began, exhibiting an uncharacteristic shyness.

"Would you like to see the pictures?" Margo asked.

In response, the girl retrieved Bear and hugged him close. "Yes, please," she whispered.

Longing to put her arms around Sooz but opting for a more casual approach, Margo led the way into the living room. The album she and Seth had gone through the night he'd turned up on her doorstep had already been installed on one of the shelves by the fireplace. He'd asked her to bring it several days earlier, pointing out that the history it contained belonged to all three of them.

Taking a seat on the couch, Margo rested the album on her knees. A bit awkwardly, Sooz settled beside her. As they began to turn the album's pages, they didn't start with Beth's baby pictures, as she and Seth had done. Instead they began at the beginning, with snapshots she'd taken of Jim during their courtship.

In particular, one taken at Snoqualmie Falls tugged at Margo's heart. The occasion had marked the first time they'd talked of marriage and the family they each wanted to have someday. Slim, dark-haired and witty, Jim had been a wonderful person. In a place reserved for him, she loved him still, though these days her tall, red-headed boat builder filled her heart.

Realizing that made it easier to describe Jim to Sooz.

"He was a police detective," she said. "Smart and funny and very courageous. He saw all kinds of terrible things in his work, yet he didn't bring them home with him. His faith in the essential goodness of human nature

remained unchanged. Whenever I think of him, I remember his smile. It could light up a room . . ."

Sooz didn't comment. "That was a pretty veil and
dress you had," she observed a few minutes later, por-
ing over their wedding photographs. "What happened to
them?"

"I kept them, thinking Beth might want to wear them
someday. They're still packed away in the attic of my
house."

Predictably, the girl clammed up when they came to the
photos Jim had taken of Margo while she was pregnant.
At five foot three, she didn't have much room between
her breasts and hips to hide the extra weight an expec-
tant mother gained. As a result, her baby-to-be had stuck
out in front rather dramatically.

That was you, Margo wanted to say as Sooz flipped
past several poses of her modeling a top printed with the
word Baby and an arrow pointing to her area of widest
girth. She longed to share the tender emotions that had
washed over her when her infant daughter had been
placed in her arms. During those fleeting, half-drugged
moments in the delivery room, the child she'd held had
been Sooz, not Beth.

It was much too soon to do anything of the sort.
They'd come a long way in just a few hours. But their
truce was fragile yet.

They were about to turn to Beth's baby pictures when
Seth came down the stairs in jeans and an old shirt. His
eyes lit with incredulity and pleasure when he saw them
sitting side by side.

"So . . . what have you ladies been up to this morning?" he asked.

Sooz's quick glance said she wasn't ready to talk to him
about what was in the album yet. As Margo quietly

closed its cover, she jumped up and gave him a hug. "We made pancake batter, Daddy," she said in her most self-important voice. "Margo says I get to cook the first batch."

At Margo's suggestion, Sooz made her pancakes silver dollar size. They were easier to turn and they browned to perfection. She glowed at Seth's high praise and chattered to him like a magpie as they ate.

Yet, though she was pleasant enough to Margo, something about the girl's attitude suggested she still viewed her as an interloper—one she expected to compete with for her father's affection. *I wonder if she'll ever accept me as a mother figure in her life?* Margo thought.

To her chagrin, as she was pouring coffee and orange juice refills, Seth mentioned their canceled honeymoon. "Though it wasn't completely scrubbed, we had less than twenty-four hours alone on San Juan," he pointed out. "I'm not willing to settle for that. It's my turn to choose, and I've thought of a completely different destination."

Margo wasn't at all sure they should leave Sooz again, at least not for quite a while. She truly wished he hadn't brought up the subject.

"Don't I get a say in this?" she asked as tactfully as she could, reluctant to air a difference of opinion in front of their pint-sized audience.

The masterful Leo man she'd married grinned and shook his head. "Nope," he answered, diving into his second plateful of pancakes with gusto. "Furthermore, I plan to keep our destination a secret. That way, nobody will be able to find us and drag us back if a certain little girl decides to run away from home again."

Already closing up like an offended mollusk at the word honeymoon, Sooz squirmed in embarrassment.

"Oh, *Daddy!*" she groaned. "You don't have to worry about that."

"I sincerely hope not, pumpkin," he relented, his eyes twinkling as he ruffled her hair.

Later, while Sooz was out playing with some friends and they were going over redecorating plans that would incorporate some of Margo's furniture, they discussed the subject in greater detail. Seth confessed he'd been thinking about Paris.

"As in *France,*" he emphasized. "That might be far enough to guarantee us some time alone."

"I really don't think we should leave Sooz for at least six months...if that soon," Margo countered. "Like the rest of us, she's been through a lot. And she's just a little girl. We need to give her ample time to adjust."

How completely unlike Cheryl she is in every respect, Seth thought, dropping a kiss on her nose. I can't imagine *her* giving up a trip to Europe because of a child's sensitivities.

"I was thinking about two weeks from now," he said. "But if you want to make it the first of April, you've got a date. You know, don't you, that after what we've been doing the past few days, if we put it off indefinitely, another little person's needs might intervene?"

They agreed on April. As the weeks passed, their combined household settled into place. Though Margo's things and Seth's were quite different, somehow they seemed to go together. The big silver-gray house overlooking the Sound had become more of a home.

Their private life went from glorious to ecstatic. Yet the close-knit relationship Margo yearned to have with Sooz continued to elude her. Polite, even friendly in a way that was hard to define, Sooz kept her distance. She didn't ask to see the album again, or mention the inadvertent baby swap that had woven their lives so intricately together. At times, Margo despaired of ever really reaching her.

At last it was time for Margo and Seth to leave on their trip. Back on the day shift at the hospital, Nell volunteered to sleep over at their house to help ease Mrs. Johnson's nervousness and both their minds. She and Sooz drove them to the airport in her station wagon.

Sooz clung tightly to her father when their flight was announced. Though she didn't offer Margo a hug, she didn't leave her new stepmother out altogether. "Have fun," she said with a quavery little smile.

Radiant in a jonquil yellow suit, Margo didn't let Seth see her worry. She was a month and a half pregnant and he was being overprotective of her. Dying to go, she still had doubts about their trip. Sooz clearly felt deserted. When they'd told her about the baby, she hadn't said very much.

Will Sooz ever really return my affection? she wondered as they boarded the plane. During our absence, will I lose the ground I've gained? How will she react when she's no longer an only child?

On their last afternoon in Paris, Seth and Margo lay partially covered by rumpled sheets in their hotel room bed. Though at the moment they were sated, she knew they probably hadn't finished making love yet. They'd have time for one more appetizer before getting showered and dressed for an early dinner at Maxim's on the Rue Royale.

Lazily Seth traced a pattern on her stomach. "It's hard to believe there's a baby in there," he said. "Your waist looks as tiny as ever."

Margo smiled fondly. "Just you wait."

A moment later, she'd turned pensive.

"What is it, sweetheart?" he asked.

"I'm worried about how Sooz is going to act when the baby's born. I don't want her to feel displaced."

He sighed. "Neither do I. No doubt if we'd had any sense, we'd have waited a while. But when you asked me not to use anything that night on San Juan, it was like setting me ablaze. I began to *crave* having a child with you."

"Selfishly speaking, I'm glad you did," Margo replied.

Neither of them said anything more for several seconds.

Then, "Maybe we're borrowing trouble," Seth allowed. "Before Cheryl and I were divorced, Sooz used to ooh and aah over every newborn and toddler that crossed her path. She actually begged us for a little brother or sister. Maybe while we've been gone, she's had a chance to think."

They slept most of the way on their overnight flight from Paris to New York, where Seth had scheduled a meeting with a business contact of his who had numerous investments and a second home in the Pacific Northwest. The result was an order for a top-of-the-line yacht that would keep the boat yard fully employed through most of the summer. They went out to dinner to celebrate, although because of the time zones they'd crossed, it felt like lunch.

Departing John F. Kennedy airport at 7:25 p.m., they reached Seattle shortly after midnight. When they arrived home by taxi, the house was silent. A single lamp had been left burning in the entry hall. Glancing at each other as they unlocked the door, they went straight upstairs to their daughter's room.

Sooz was fast asleep. In the dim light from the hall, she looked almost angelic. Seth had a fleeting impression something was missing from the peaceful, familiar scene, but he couldn't put his finger on exactly what it was.

I wonder where we stand, Margo thought as she gazed at the girl with affection. I know Sooz isn't angry with me anymore. But will she ever accept me as a second mother?

From the guest room, they could hear Nell's gentle snores. "We need to come up with a special treat to thank her," Margo whispered. "She's been a wonderful friend to us."

It wasn't until they entered their own room that Seth realized what had been bothering him. Warm feelings flooded them both at the welcome Nell and Sooz had prepared.

Constructed of shelving paper and lettered in red marking pen, a huge Welcome Home banner stretched from one side of their headboard to the other. Sooz's customary bed partner, Bear, was seated regally on Seth's pillow with a red ribbon around his neck and a hand-lettered sign that read Official Hugger and Greeter.

Margo's pillow hadn't gone begging. Propped on it was a framed picture, drawn in crayon by the child she'd learned to love so much. It depicted a man and a woman with their arms around a little girl. The man had red hair, while the woman and girl had been given dark, springy curls. Behind them, the sun was shining. The girl held a baby wrapped in a pink bunting in her arms.

*   *   *   *   *

LOVE AND
THE LEO MAN

by Wendy Corsi Staub

While the dog days of August may seem unbearable to some people, chances are the Leo man is perfectly content. After all, his sign is ruled by the sun, and he basks in its blazing summer heat. Hardly a homebody, this confident, friendly fellow can often be found at the beach or park, where his sunny personality ensures that he won't be alone for long. He radiates a warmth that's irresistible to the opposite sex, but once he's found Miss Right, he'll be utterly devoted!

In Suzanne Carey's BABY SWAP sexy Leo man Seth Danner is smitten by the enigmatic, clever Gemini woman Margo Rourke. For her, he'd do anything—even spend a glorious summer day reading books under a shade tree— as long as they can be together. How would YOU and the Leo man spend the long, hot days of August?

The *Aries* woman, whose energy knows no bounds, is likely to pick the steamiest month of the year for some rigorous mountain hiking. The Leo man will be with her every step of the way, even in the most rugged terrain. And when they reach the top, where the air is pleasantly brisk and the view majestic, he'll truly feel like a king with the world at his feet ... and his love at his side.

The Leo man knows his *Taurus* darling is a pushover when it comes to desserts, and he loves to treat her to all her favorite confections. To help her cool off when the mercury rises, he'll stock up on gallons of ice cream in a rainbow of flavors. After indulging to her heart's content, she'll thank him with the sweetest of kisses!

When the pavement is broiling and the air conditioner is on the blink, the Leo man will have the ideal escape for the *Cancer* woman. Born in a water sign, she adores the sea—he'll be delighted when he whisks her aboard a borrowed sailboat! Nothing could be closer to heaven than a day spent skimming the waves, enjoying the salty spray and exhilarating breeze—together!

There's no question what two *Leo* lovebirds will have planned when temperatures soar—a day at the beach, of course! These professional sunbathers will pack the car with all the essentials: sodas and snacks, lotions and oils, volleyball equipment, a radio, even snorkeling gear! Arriving early will allow them to stake their umbrella in the heart of the action, and since they're true romantics, they'll stay to watch the sunset!

The Leo man is charmed by his *Virgo* woman's ladylike demeanor, and he'll surprise her with a delicate Victorian lace fan when the weather becomes muggy. He'll be content to while away the long, lazy hours together, rocking gently on her porch swing as classical music drifts through the open windows. They'll sip lemonade from frosty glasses ... and dreamily discuss their future!

The *Libra* woman was born to shop, so when it's hot and sticky outdoors, she's bound to head *indoors* to the air-conditioned comfort of the mall! The Leo man will browse alongside her as she searches for sales and bargains, and he'll wait by dressing room doors—knowing his patience will be rewarded when she models her new summer wardrobe, complete with miniskirts and bikinis!

The Leo man knows that the *Scorpio* woman will make a beeline for the pool when a heat wave strikes—and she's likely to stay there for hours. Hers is a water sign, and she knows nothing is more refreshing on a hazy, humid August day than a swim. The Leo man is always happy to dive in with her—especially on those steamy nights when a midnight skinny dip is irresistible!

No one is more fun-loving than the vivacious *Sagittarius* woman, and the Leo man will really make her smile when he tells her his plans for a sunny summer Saturday: a day at the amusement park! They'll ride every ride, fill up on cotton candy, and because the Leo man is truly in love, he'll stay at the ringtoss booth until he's won his lady the biggest, cutest teddy bear prize!

The ambitious *Capricorn* woman will insist on going to the office, even on the most beautiful summer day. But the Leo man will show up right before her lunch hour, bearing a wicker basket brimming with goodies. They'll share a picnic for two under a tree in the park, where the persuasive Leo man will convince his love that taking the rest of the afternoon off is a terrific idea!

The *Aquarius* woman is truly a free spirit, and the Leo man is usually game to go along with her adventures in the name of love. When the weather at home becomes too sticky for comfort, she'll spontaneously purchase two tickets to Alaska, and the Leo man won't blink an eye! After all, it's a surefire way to beat the heat and enjoy a romantic getaway with the love of his life!

The creative *Pisces* woman loves drama, fantasy...*and* her dashing Leo man. In her opinion there's no better way to escape the blazing August heat than in an air-conditioned movie theater with her mate at her side. If they're *really* lucky, they'll be able to see a romantic classic, and she'll sigh contentedly in between bites of popcorn, cuddling up to her own real live hero!

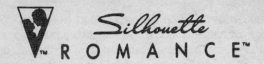

Silhouette

ROMANCE™

COMING NEXT MONTH

#886   A CHANGED MAN—Karen Leabo   *Written in the Stars*
Conservative Virgo man Stephen Whitfield was too uptight for
impulsive Sagittarius Jill Ballantine. But Jill sensed a lovable man
beneath that stuffy accountant exterior. All Stephen needed was a
little loosening up!

#887   WILD STREAK—Pat Tracy
Erin Clay had always been off-limits to Linc Severance—first as his
best friend's wife and then as his best friend's widow. Now Linc was
back in town . . . and ready to test the forbidden waters.

#888   YOU MADE ME LOVE YOU—Jayne Addison
Nothing Caroline Phelps ever did seemed to turn out right—*except*
meeting sexy Jack Corey. But when life's little disasters began to
occur, could Caroline trust Jack to always be there?

#889   JUST ONE OF THE GUYS—Jude Randal
Dana Morgan was a do-it-yourself woman—more at home in a
hardware store than in a beauty parlor. But Spencer Willis was out to
prove there *was* one thing Dana couldn't do alone . . . fall in love!

#890   MOLLY MEETS HER MATCH—Val Whisenand
To Molly Evans, Brian Forrester was a gorgeous male specimen. So
what if he was in a wheelchair? But she *couldn't* ignore his stubborn
pride—or his passion . . . even if she wanted to.

#891   THE IDEAL WIFE—Joleen Daniels
Sloan Burdett wanted Lacey Sue Talbert like no woman on earth, but
if he was going to have her, he'd have to move fast. Lacey Sue was
about to walk down the aisle with his brother. . . .

AVAILABLE THIS MONTH:

#880   BABY SWAP
Suzanne Carey

#881   THE WIFE HE WANTED
Elizabeth August

**#882   HOME IS WHERE THE
HEART IS**
Carol Grace

**#883   LAST CHANCE FOR
MARRIAGE**
Sandra Paul

#884   FIRE AND SPICE
Carla Cassidy

**#885   A HOLIDAY TO
REMEMBER**
Brittany Young

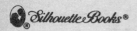

Take 4 bestselling love stories FREE

Plus get a FREE surprise gift!

Silhouette
R O M A N C E™

★ WRITTEN IN THE STARS ★

WHEN A VIRGO MAN MEETS A SAGITTARIUS WOMAN

Accountant Stephen Whitfield's aunt was being swindled and it was all Jill Ballantine's fault! Straitlaced Stephen had never been able to get along with his free-spirited cousin by marriage—she'd always known how to make him lose control. But now Jill wanted Stephen to lose his heart…to her! There's a cosmic attraction in Karen Leabo's A CHANGED MAN, coming in September, only from Silhouette Romance. It's WRITTEN IN THE STARS!